HER DESERT PROTECTOR

MARIE TUHART

Trifecta Publishing House who took a chance on this series

DEAR READER

The country of Bashir is a fictional place. They have their own customs and different rules for titles.

The title of Lady before someone's name is a sign of respect and not an official title.

In all the books, once the heroine is engaged to the hero they will become princess-to-be and when they marry, they will carry the princess title.

I have taken liberties in creating my own country, it is a progressive country and looking toward the future.

Published in the United States of America First Printing: 2019

Print

ISBN -13: 978-1-943407-62-0

E-Book

ISBN -13: 978-1-943407-61-3

Trifecta Publishing House

1120 East 6th Street

Port Angeles, Washington

98362

Contact Information: Info@TrifectaPublishingHouse.com

Editor: Elizabeth Jewell

Cover Art by Designed by Diana

Formatted by Monica Corwin

Zoey Lacey bit into the ripe apple with a crunch and closed her eyes in awe of the sweet taste exploding on her tongue. She hadn't tasted an apple this good in a while. She smiled at the vendor before she continued her journey through the marketplace in Bashir City. There was row after row of merchants, from fruit and vegetable vendors to those offering the heady scents of spices, shoes and clothing, furniture and electronics. Excitement slid through her veins.

She'd come to the country of Bashir because of its 300th anniversary. It would make a good story, not only for her travel blog, but also an article she hoped to sell to a magazine.

Some might say Zoey was crazy to wander the world, taking pictures, writing stories, never having a steady paycheck, but she loved it. After a childhood with overprotective parents, she enjoyed being out on her own and doing what she wanted. She finished her apple and dropped the core into a garbage bin.

A smile played around her lips as a group of children ran past her. Bashir City was one of the cleanest cities she'd ever visited. The people were friendly, but it helped that she spoke Arabic, even though most of them spoke English as well. Most were surprised and delighted when she spoke to them in their native tongue.

Zoey turned the corner and automatically brought her camera up. She snapped picture after picture of the buildings, the blend of old and new architecture delighting her as she wandered down the roadway.

She stopped beside one of the apartment buildings. The iron balcony caused a smile to cross her lips. She'd seen one like this only in New Orleans. The white shutters were closed to keep out the sun. What really caught her attention was the intricate graffiti on one wall. She stared at the blend of colors and designs. Could it be a symbol for something? She took several pictures before starting out again.

The hair on the back of Zoey's neck stood up. She slipped her backpack around front and placed her camera inside it. As she slid it back into place she looked over her shoulder. She didn't see anyone, but she'd learned never to ignore her instincts. Young male voices sounded behind her. She could only make out a word or two: woman and alone. Plus their laughter.

Zoey picked up her pace and forced herself to keep her breathing steady, her hands loose at her side. Judging by the voices, there were at least four of them. Not good odds if they decided to come after her, but she'd learned from the best how to defend herself. Six months in war-torn Iraq would do that to a person.

Turning the corner of the next building, she ran into a male chest. Fear slid up her spine as her breath whooshed out. "So sorry," she said, starting to sidestep him.

"Are you all right?" She glanced up to see black short hair, dark eyes, hair and stern features. His rough, husky voice sent shivers down her spine.

Yet there was concern in his dark eyes.

"Fine."

She turned her head when she heard swearing. The four boys had rounded the corner. Young twenty-somethings, or at least that's what she thought. They stared at her with wide eyes and frowns. Before she could ask what they wanted, they turned and ran.

"Stay here," the man commanded before he stepped around her and took off after the boys.

Zoey turned, rounded the corner, and watched him chase after the boys. She was about to go after him when another man came out of the door of the building and walked toward her.

"Ma'am," he said. His dark brown hair was cut close to his head. His posture screamed military.

"American?" She was surprised. She hadn't run into many of her fellow countrymen here.

"Yes, ma'am, I'm Ryan. If you would please come with me," he said, gesturing toward the building.

"To where?" She wasn't about to jump into the fire. She had no clue who this man was.

"Just inside. Khalid radioed me. He wants to be sure you're safe." Ryan paused. "We're local security, please."

"Khalid?"

Ryan waved in the direction the stranger had taken off in. The brooding, way-too-handsome stranger whose eyes had mesmerized her. Zoey shook her head. She bristled, then reminded herself that she was a visitor, and if this was local security ... "May I see some ID, please?"

His eyebrows rose, but he fished a leather case out of his pocket and held it out to her.

She took it and opened it.

Ryan Andrews.

Team leader.

Bashir Independent Security Force.

There was his picture and a badge that looked official. "Wait a second, you said local security, but this says you're independent security."

"Yes, ma'am. Bashir's police force is independent from the royal security force."

She studied him. Her instincts told her he was telling her the truth, but still she was leery.

"Please, ma'am. Come inside. We will be out of the hot sun, and I can get your statement. I promise no harm will come to you. You have my word."

That made sense. "Very well." Together they walked up the stairs and inside what turned out to be no ordinary building. The room was huge. Several men sat around watching monitors. If she squinted, she could make out different shots of the street outside. "I've never seen anything like this outside of the military."

"As most of this is private security, I suspect you haven't." Ryan led her across the room and gestured to the table and chairs. "Have a seat. Khalid should return shortly."

"I thought you were going to take my statement?"

His cheeks turned ruddy, but his blue eyes twinkled. "Not just yet. Khalid will want to hear what you have to say. So please, sit and relax. I'll get you some water."

What the hell? He'd all but ordered her into the place, and now he was waiting for the stranger to return. She wrinkled her nose at him as he walked away. Zoey took off her pack and set it on the table. What had she stumbled into? And who was the dark-haired, dark-eyed man who had taken after those boys?

Khalid al-Hakim swore as he made his way back to the new surveillance center. The group of boys had gotten away. Were they part of Kalif's group? Kalif, Bashir's resident drug lord, was growing bolder and more dangerous with each passing day. Khalid, his family, and his security forces had destroyed all but the main poppy field, which still existed mainly because they couldn't seem to find the damn thing. That didn't stop Kalif from recruiting more men or, should he say, more young men. The ones Khalid had chased couldn't be more than twenty, if that.

Khalid marched into the building, his gaze sweeping the room. There she was, sitting at the table with a bottle of water clenched in her hand, observing everything going on around her. He stood there for a moment.

He'd noticed her on the security cameras they'd installed around the area. He'd been intrigued from the moment he'd seen her. The way she walked, with confidence and grace. The way she handled her camera spoke of both training and enjoyment. Her red hair, pulled back away from her face, made him take notice of her full lips and strong chin. Then there were those long legs. He wondered what they would feel like wrapped around his waist.

He shook his head. Where did that thought come from? He admired how she paid attention to her surroundings, and to have realized she was being followed spoke to some training or at least very honed instincts.

Khalid hadn't intended to run into her. He'd taken the side entrance and planned to walk past her, but he hadn't expected her to come barreling around the corner and straight into him.

His cock had jumped when her soft body landed against his, an odd reaction for him. Not that he didn't like women, but usually it took a while before his dick got into the action. Khalid let out a sigh.

Now was not the time. No matter how much his body wanted her. Shaking his thoughts away and willing his body under control, he strode over to her.

Their gazes clashed, and Khalid halted in his tracks. Her eyes were ... silver. There was no other color to describe them.

"Are you going to stand there staring?" There was irritation in her voice, and his lips curved into a smile. Most people would be nervous, but not this woman. She might be angry, yet she was a study in calm steadiness.

"I apologize." Khalid pulled out a chair and sat down before holding out his hand. "Khalid, head of security."

"I never would have guessed." His rough hand encased her soft one.

If he hadn't been paying close attention, he would never have noticed the small shiver that went through her body. "Are you all right?" He released her hand when she tugged and instantly missed her warmth.

"Fine. I take it you didn't catch the young men?"

"No. They disappeared. Any idea why they were following you?"

She shrugged her shoulders. "They were just young men. Probably wanted to flirt with me." She tilted her head.

"Then why chase you?"

She shrugged her shoulders, and Khalid frowned at her attitude. "Are you American?"

"Yes. I'm Zoey." Her cheeks turned pink. "I should have told you my name before."

"What are you doing in Bashir?" He forced himself not to react to the way her soft voice soothed over his skin, sinking into his bones.

"I'm a travel writer, and I'm here for the anniversary party."

"May I see your passport?" It would only take him a few minutes to identify how she had come into the country.

She regarded him with those silver eyes of hers. "I guess." She unzipped the pocket of her cargo pants and pulled out a small blue book. "I trust you'll bring this right back to me?"

"I will. You have my word." Distrust reflected in her eyes, and he patiently waited.

She let out a sigh and held her passport out to him.

"Thank you. I'll be right back." He slid back his chair, rose, and crossed the room to where Ryan stood next to the computers, his back straight as he stared at the screen showing the front of the building.

"Well?" Ryan asked.

"She says she's here for the anniversary party." He gave Jahir, his resident computer guru, the passport. Within a minute, Zoey's information was up on the screen. Zoey Lacey, US resident, twenty-seven years old, had cleared customs just this morning, and flown in from Iraq.

Ryan whistled. "Iraq?"

"Says she's a travel writer," Khalid answered.

Jahir's fingers flew over the keyboard. "She is," Jahir said, "according to this." He waved his hand at the screen. "She freelances for several different magazines and writes a very popular travel blog." He pulled up her blog.

There were all the normal travel pictures until Jahir scrolled down further, and Khalid's mouth dropped open.

There was a picture of an Iraqi village, one that had been bombed out. The empty village, shelled-out buildings, and a mother and child sitting in the street. The picture was haunting and tragic, but also beautiful.

"She is very good," Ryan said.

"So it seems." Khalid picked the passport up. "Since I'm not sure if those were just local boys or part of Kalif's group, let's escort her to where she's staying. I want to make sure she's not being watched."

"You think she's a target for Kalif to grab?" Ryan asked.

Kalif would grab women to keep his men happy. "There is no reason to think so, but I'd rather be safe." He turned and walked back over to Zoey, who sat watching him. "Here you go." He handed her passport back to her.

"I assume I check out?" Her voice held a slight hint of laughter.

"Yes. Ryan and I will escort you to where you're staying."

"That's really not necessary." She stood, slipping her backpack on. "I have more photos to take."

"Not today."

Her eyes flashed anger. Why was she angry? "We will escort you." He used his stern voice, the one he used when his family didn't want to listen.

"Look, there is no need. I'm not done with the job I came to do."

"Neither am I." He stared at her, trying not to grin at the mutinous expression on her face. "I can put you under protective custody if you won't cooperate." Her express grew darker and he prepared himself for a fight. "I only want to make sure you're safe in my country."

She let out a heavy sigh. "Whatever." She rolled her eyes before stepping around the table and striding toward the entrance of the building.

Khalid jogged a couple of steps to catch up with her. "Where are you staying?"

"I figured you already knew that. Bashir City Palm Resort."

He almost laughed. The hotel was not a resort, but it was clean and safe. Babak was a good man and made sure his guests were well taken care of. "It is a nice place."

Zoey shrugged, ignoring her escorts as she moved with purpose down the sidewalk. Within fifteen minutes they stood outside the hotel.

"Thank you for the escort."

"We will see you to your room."

"Afraid I'll run away the second you leave me?"

"No." He pushed open the door and held it for her. With a shrug, Zoey walked past him.

"Ah, Miss Lacey. You have returned." His smile was genuine, but when he saw Khalid it faded a little. "Pr--"

"Babak," Khalid said before the man could say his title. "Miss Lacey here ran into a little trouble with a couple of the local boys. All is fine, but I decided she needed an escort back to your establishment."

"Yes, of course." His gaze bounced between Zoey and Khalid. "I have your room ready, Miss Lacey. Let me get your bag." Babak disappeared, then returned with a large rolling duffel bag.

"Thank you." Zoey reached for her bag.

Khalid reached around her and snatched it up.

She stared at him and gave him a tight smile as Babak handed her the key to her room. The trio walked over to the elevator. "Look, I'm not comfortable with strange men walking me to my room."

"Then it's a good thing you know who we are."

"That's not funny." She crossed her arms over her chest.

"Babak," he called.

"Yes, sir." Babak came over to them.

"Would you please vouch for Ryan and myself to Miss Lacey? She's not sure if she should allow us to accompany her to her room."

"Oh. Miss Lacey, Khalid and Ryan are upstanding ... citizens ... and they protect those of us in Bashir. There is no reason not to trust them."

Zoey threw up her hands. "I know when I'm beat," she muttered as the elevator doors opened. "Thank you, Babak." She stepped inside the elevator, and they followed.

"I can take it," she said when she punched the button for the third floor.

"My mother would faint if I didn't carry a lady's bags for her."

Ryan snickered and Khalid shot him a look, but Ryan ignored him. When the elevator's door opened, Khalid waited for Zoey to get out.

"Room three-ten." She turned to the left and found the correct door.

Khalid plucked the key from her fingers and opened the door. "Stay here. I'm going to make sure it's safe." He stepped into the room. Within a couple of minutes, he gestured for her to enter.

"You take precautions to a new level," she commented as she passed him.

Khalid couldn't help but grin. "Making sure your room is secure."

Zoey shook her head, but worry flashed over her features. He wanted nothing more than to gather her into his arms and make sure she stayed safe. He barely knew this woman, but his protective instincts were on high. Why?

"It is." She dropped her backpack on the bed and turned to stare at him. "I'm safe now, and you can be on your way." She waved her hands in the air.

"Do you have a mobile phone?"

"Yes." She stood without moving.

"May I see it, please?" Khalid held out his hand. This woman was suspicious of everything. Not that it was a bad thing.

"Why?"

He took a deep breath. "I'd like to make sure you have our local emergency numbers in case you need them."

She unzipped the pocket of her backpack, pulled her phone out, and dangled it in her fingers.

He plucked it from her. "Hey," she protested.

He unlocked the phone since she had no security on it, found the contacts, and input his name and number. "If you have any problems or issues, call." He handed her back her phone.

"I won't need to." Her tone was firm as she lifted her chin and stared at him, feet apart as if ready for a fight. He wanted to chuckle at her stance.

"I hope not." He turned and left the room with Ryan following.

Zoey shook her head as she shut the door and locked it behind her escorts. She disliked overprotective men; she'd had enough of that growing up. Though Khalid's dark looks sure added to his air of mystique, and also made her heart pound. There was something about his commanding voice that made her shiver.

She rolled her eyes. Pushing all thoughts of Khalid out of her head, Zoey slipped off her backpack and put it on the bed, then picked up her duffel and set it on the luggage rack, opening it to pull out clean clothes.

A quick shower and then she'd download the photos she'd taken today and make sure everything was backed up to the cloud. She glanced at her watch. After she did that, it would be time for dinner.

Zoey worked for a few hours until her stomach protested. She hadn't eaten much that day. An early flight from Iraq had meant a quick breakfast, and she'd only grabbed that apple for lunch.

Picking up her backpack, she made her way out to the street and began walking. The sun was still out, but it was not as hot as before. People were making their way home from their jobs or to the market-place to get supplies for dinner. She stopped in front of a small restaurant. Mashawai's, the sign said. It was like a lot of the buildings, a mixture of old and new. Older stone facades, but the awning and signage were new.

She glanced at the menu in the window, then peeked inside. This was a nice-looking, quaint restaurant. It was small, holding no more than maybe ten tables. It appeared to be family run, and several locals were dining there. She loved eating where the locals did.

She stepped inside. The smell of roasting lamb filled the air, along with spices. Her mouth watered.

"Welcome to Mashawai's. Table for one?" a young woman in a long green dress greeted her.

"Yes, please." Zoey followed the young woman to a simple wood table, covered by a white cloth, and with a menu, napkin, and utensils already set out. Zoey pulled out the chair and sat down.

"Your waiter will be right here. Please enjoy your meal." The young woman walked away.

Zoey placed the napkin in her lap and picked up the menu. Every-thing was listed in Arabic and English, which was good. Her reading of Arabic wasn't the best.

"Good evening, I'm Yasir, your waiter. Would you like something to drink?"

Zoey glanced up. She noticed the resemblance between the waiter and the hostess who had seated her. Her guess was right about the place being run by a family. He also wore a pair of green pants the same shade as the hostess's dress and a white shirt.

"Fruit juice."

"We have several; how about a nice pineapple and melon blend?" he suggested.

"Sounds perfect." She set her menu down. "What do you recommend for dinner?"

His dark brown eyes widened, and she hid a smile. He wasn't expecting her to ask that. "For an appetizer, tabbouleh; main dish, shawarma; and for dessert, pistachio and walnut baklava."

Already Zoey's mouth was watering. "Sounds perfect." She grinned at the waiter.

"I'll have the fruit juice and tabbouleh right out." He picked up her menu and hurried away.

Zoey pulled a small notebook out of her backpack and made some notes. She had a good memory, but she still liked to jot things down. Once that was done, she dug out her phone. She'd found her blog readers loved when she'd share pictures of the food she'd eaten.

Yasir strode up to the table with a bowl and a pitcher of juice. He poured her a glass and set the bowl of tabbouleh in front of her. "If you need anything, don't hesitate to ask."

"Thank you." After taking a photo, Zoey lifted her fork and took a bite. The mint burst upon her tongue, then the sweet taste of onion. The bulgur and tomatoes rounded out the dish. The spices were subtle.

A shadow fell across her table. She looked up and her eyes widened. Khalid stood there.

"I see you didn't stay in your room," he said.

She sat straighter in her chair. "Are you following me?" She winced at her accusing tone. "Sorry, that was rude."

"You can make it up to me by allowing me to join you." He gestured to the empty chair.

Zoey nodded and he sat down. "And to answer your question, I saw you sitting here alone and thought you might like some company."

Part of her was suspicious, but another part of her was glad for the company. Hell, her woman parts had gone all perky and hard the moment he spoke. What was it about this commanding man that attracted her so?

She popped the last bite into her mouth as Yasir came rushing over with another place setting and poured him a glass of juice. "It's a honor to have you here--"

"Thank you, Yasir."

Zoey stared at Khalid. He liked cutting people off. Why was that? What was he afraid they might say? She liked puzzles, though this particular one might be more interesting than most.

"What may I get for you, sir?" Yasir asked.

"I'll have whatever Miss Lacey is having." Yasir nodded and left. He turned his attention to her, and Zoey found herself drowning in his eyes.

"So, Khalid, what do you do when you're not escorting women to their hotel rooms or checking out their credentials or following them to restaurants?"

He laughed and that husky chuckle flowed through her veins. "As I said earlier, I'm head of security."

"Yes, but security of what? The city? The country?" Something flashed in his eyes and Zoey bit back a grin. So he was hiding something.

"The security of the people of Bashir." He picked up his glass and took a sip.

"That's a big job."

"You have no idea."

Yasir walked up to the table with the shawarma. The meat was in a wrap, along with lettuce and tomato. Zoey snapped another photo, then picked up the hot wrap and took a small bite. *Oh, my goodness.* The garlic filled her senses. It was delicious. The lamb was tender and moist.

"Why did you take a picture of your food before you took a bite?" Khalid waved his hand at her phone.

Should she answer with the same elusiveness as Khalid? The man was basically a stranger, but Zoey had always preferred to play it straight. Besides, he actually looked interested. "For my blog. My readers enjoy seeing pictures of the food in the places I travel to."

He took a bite of his own food and looked thoughtful. "Do you enjoy doing your travel blog?"

"Yes." She ate a few more bites, the meat practically melting on her tongue. Then she sipped her fruit juice and, without taking her attention from him, she made a few notes in her journal.

Odd how she couldn't take her attention from him. Maybe it was because she was enjoying his company even if he was a little controlling. He finished off his food, and she wondered how long it had been since he had last eaten.

"I am enjoying doing the blog." She grinned. "But if I don't take notes, I won't remember everything. The tastes, the smell, the experience." She polished off her meal.

"Did you enjoy it?" Yasir asked as he removed their plates.

"Very much so. My compliments to the cook."

Yasir beamed at her. "Father will be happy to hear that. Your desserts will be right out."

Zoey groaned. "I'll never be able to eat dessert." She was full now, so maybe she'd eat a bite or two and take the rest back to her hotel room.

"I thought all women loved dessert, no matter what."

"I do." Zoey took a sip of the juice. "But I'm stuffed."

Khalid regarded her with disbelief shining in his eyes. "You barely ate anything."

"I ate an appetizer, and then the main course. The food is very filling, and I have to keep in shape."

"I think your shape is just fine."

Heat flared over her skin.

Yasir arrived, carrying the plate of baklava and accompanied by an older man dressed very much like him. She saw the resemblance, even thought the older man's face was lined with age. "This is my father. He wanted to say thank you for the compliment on the food."

Zoey nodded. "It is all very delicious," she said in Arabic. "You are a great cook."

The man's brown eyes widened, and he smiled. He reached over and took her hand and kissed the back of it, all the while telling her she was beautiful and he was glad she graced his restaurant with her presence. Then he looked at the man sitting with her and gave a deep bow before he left.

Yasir was shaking his head as his father walked away. "You made his day. Not many Americans speak Arabic."

"How did you know I'm American?" She wondered what that bow to Khalid meant. It seemed very odd the older man hadn't spoken to him.

"No accent." Yasir walked away, and Zoey laughed.

"Do I really not have an accent?" she asked Khalid.

"You don't, but you are very fluent in our language." He cocked his head. "Why?"

"In my travels it's good to have a basic knowledge of local languages, but when I was in Iraq I picked up quite a bit." She picked up one of the triangle-shaped baklava and put it into her mouth. The combination of pistachio and walnuts, with honey, sugar, and syrup, made her sweet tooth sit up and take notice.

Khalid stared at her as she swallowed. A shiver of awareness slid over her skin. Khalid finished off the baklava he'd put on his dish. After three more tastes, she pushed the plate away. "I can't eat another bite."

There were still six more pieces, but she couldn't. Yasir grinned as he took the plate to box up what was left.

"What are your plans after dinner?" Khalid asked.

"What are you offering?" Zoey closed her eyes as her face heated. What the hell did she just blurt out? Her mouth was running away with her thoughts today.

He laughed. "I would be honored to show you around the town."

She tilted her head and studied him. "Afraid to leave me alone?"

"No. I thought you might like a tour of sorts."

"That is very nice of you." It was a lovely gesture, but probably not wise, given her attraction to him. She needed some distance. "I really need to get back to my hotel room and work. So maybe another time." Yasir placed the box on the table.

"I hope you enjoy your stay here in Bashir, and please come back to Mashawai's." He turned to walk away.

"Yasir, I need my bill." She would never leave without paying.

Yasir looked at Khalid. "It's been take care of." He scurried off.

Zoey turned her gaze to Khalid. "Now, how did you manage to cover the bill when you haven't left this table?"

"Yasir and I have an understanding when I come to Mashawai's to eat."

Zoey glared at Khalid. "I can pay for my own meals."

"I'm sure you can." He reached out and covered her hand where it lay on the table. "Allow me this one small favor."

His tone was soft and eager. In a way he was telling her and not asking her, which irritated her. "All right, but you've used up your allotted favors." She pulled out her wallet. "But I'm leaving the tip." Zoey laid several bills on the table. Then she picked up her backpack and the box of baklava. "Thank you for keeping me company."

"I enjoyed it." Khalid rose to his feet.

"Have a nice evening." Zoey walked to the entrance with Khalid following her. Not a good idea. Those dark eyes called to her, and if she got him near her hotel room again ... She held her hand up. "I'm fine walking by myself."

Khalid looked as if he wanted to argue, but instead he nodded and leaned against the building, watchful as always. Zoey took several steps, but couldn't help glancing over her shoulder at him.

His eyes were on her. She crossed the street and went into her hotel. Who knew being watched like that could be so darned erotic? Her heart pounded with awareness. Her whole body tingled. In her room, she glanced out the window to see him walk off. Maybe she should give him a chance if they met again.

After such a good meal, she wanted to sleep, but she'd do some more work tonight, then sleep. Better to start tomorrow on top of her work. She didn't like to run behind, especially in a foreign country.

~

Khalid was going over parade route maps for Bashir's anniversary party. Security could use the police force to help on the streets, but they were going to need sharpshooters.

His stomach tightened. He didn't want to pull in more specialized sharpshooters. So many things could go wrong, but he had to do what was right to protect his family and the people of Bashir. He'd have Ryan put out some feelers and get his input. It would only be for a short period of time.

Khalid's cell phone vibrated where it lay on his desk. He looked at the time; it was almost four in the morning. Who would be calling him? He glanced at the number. Zoey. She'd been on his mind since yesterday. Maybe she'd been thinking of him too, but it was so early. "Khalid here."

"Ummm, it's Zoey." She was a bit out of breath, and he heard a slight tremor in her voice.

"Is something wrong?" His heart pounded.

"Yeah, sort of. I think you'd better get to my hotel room. The local police are here, and they're not happy with me."

"What?" Khalid jumped out of his chair and headed for the door. "Put the ranking officer on the phone."

He found Ryan in the office kitchen brewing coffee. Khalid began speaking before Ryan even looked up. "We need to get to the hotel. Something has happened."

"What? Where?" Ryan asked.

"Zoey. The local police are in her hotel room."

"What did she do?" Ryan asked as they strode down the hallway to the front door.

"At four in the morning, I have no clue. I'm waiting to talk to the ranking officer."

Ryan nodded, opening the front door, and they made their way to the SUV parked in front.

A voice came on the line. "Officer Saleem speaking."

"Officer Saleem, this is Prince Khalid, what is going on? Is Zoey all right?"

"Sir, ummm, Prin—"

"No title." Khalid cut him off. He didn't want Zoey to know he was part of the royal family. It was better she didn't. "What happened?"

"Someone broke into Miss Lacey's room. We have him in custody, but he swears it's his room."

"Where is Babak?"

"He'll be here any minute."

"I'll be there in ten minutes. Do not let the man go. Make sure Miss Lacey is comfortable until I arrive." Khalid ended the call. Another attack on Zoey? What the hell was going on?

They made it to Bashir City in record time. The roads were practically deserted, which made sense with it being so early in the morning. When the SUV pulled up in front of the hotel, Khalid bailed out and ran up the stairs to Zoey's room.

"I'm telling you he's lying." Zoey's irate voice carried into the hall.

Khalid entered the room. Two officers stood next to a young man who rubbed his head. Zoey was toe-to-toe with Officer Saleem, who looked very uncomfortable. Zoey, on the other hand, looked delicious in shorts and a tank top, her tan skin glowing in the light. "Will someone tell me what is going on?"

Eyes turned to him.

"Intruder," Zoey said.

"We don't know that," Officer Saleem said.

Khalid looked at Ryan, who was with Babak. "Babak, this is Miss Lacey's room, is it not?"

"Yes, sir."

"Told you." Zoey put her hands on her hips.

Khalid hid his smile and glanced at the intruder, who was looking at the floor, his shoulders slumped; he was shuffling his feet, but still rubbing his head. "What is wrong with him?"

"I hit him over the head." She gestured to the broken lamp on the floor. "Sorry, Babak. I'll pay for the damage."

"What?" Khalid shook his head before taking Zoey's hands in his. The slight trembling of her body made him want to comfort her. "You and I need to talk about your doing crazy things." He released her hands to place his palms on her shoulders, enjoying the feel of her soft skin. "Are you okay?"

"I'm fine." She shifted from one foot to the other, but the trembling stopped. "I woke to the sound of glass breaking." She indicated the window. "I saw this guy climbing through the window, so I grabbed the lamp and hit him with it."

Khalid glanced at the intruder, then to Officer Saleem. "Officer Saleem, if you would please take this young man down to the station, I'll join you there shortly."

"Yes, sir." They hustled the man out of the room.

Glass crunched under his feet. He looked down, noticing Zoey's uncovered feet. Why hadn't someone gotten her a pair of shoes? "You need shoes."

"I need to know why that kid broke in here."

"We'll find out."

"I'll go get another room for Miss Lacey," Babak said.

"No need, Babak. Miss Lacey will be coming with me."

2

"Like hell," Zoey whispered. But Khalid didn't react defensively. Instead, he moved closer to her.

"You can step away now." She put her hands on his shoulders as if to push him away.

He looked down at her. Her silver eyes were glowing with wariness and anger. "Maybe I don't want to." Where the hell did those words come from? He had no idea, and didn't have the time to think that through right now. Still, he found they were true. She looked perfect surrounded by him, like a lover waiting for a kiss.

"I ... " Her fingers curled around his shoulders.

"The danger may not be over." More and more, Khalid believed Kalif was somehow behind this. And Kalif was crafty. If one of his spies had caught sight of Zoey with Khalid, she could be a target. While it was a long shot, he wasn't willing to take the chance.

"Really?" She tilted her head, and he fought the urge to lean down and kiss the exposed skin of her neck. "The guy was alone as far as I could tell, and I want to know who he is and why he was in my room."

"Good question." Khalid reined in his libido. "Stay here and don't move. There is glass everywhere." He pushed away from her tempting body and moved to her duffel bag. He pulled out socks, pants, and a top, then returned to her and put them into her arms. "Let's get you dressed." He lifted her into his arms.

"Khalid," she cried.

"I don't want you cutting your feet." He carried her into the minuscule bathroom and set her down. "Dress and then we'll go." He turned to shut the door behind him.

"Wait a second." Zoey dropped her clothes on the counter. "I don't need to go with you. I'm perfectly fine here at the hotel. Babak said he'd give me another room."

"The break-in proves that false."

"Seriously." She crossed her arms over her breasts. "I'm pretty sure it was a random act, but until the police interview him, I won't know for sure."

"Random at four in the morning?" He shook his head. "You will do this my way." He pulled the door shut behind him.

Zoey took a deep breath when Khalid left the room. The man was over-the-top protective. It bothered her, yet he made every nerve in her body tingle with excitement. But he wasn't the man for her. It was obvious he was used to being obeyed, and she rebelled against certain authority.

Stepping out of her shorts, she slipped on her pants and pulled her top on over her tank. She sat on the toilet and put on her socks, then opened the door. Khalid was there with her boots.

Without a word, she took them and slipped them on, glaring at him. "I don't take orders well." Yet she was obeying him. Irritation flowed through her veins as she lifted her chin, but she didn't step farther into the room.

"Who would do such a thing?" Babak's voice held astonishment. "I'm so sorry, Miss Lacey. I have no idea how this could have happened." There was anger in his voice.

"It's not your fault, Babak." Zoey wanted to comfort the man, but Khalid stood close to her and if she moved, she was sure he'd stop her. Looking at him, she said, "I don't need to go with you, I'm fine here."

"No." Khalid glared at her, but she didn't care.

"Listen," she started.

"Babak, let's go find something to close that window up with and clean up the glass." Ryan took the man by the arm, led him out of the room, and closed the door behind him.

"Ryan is a smart man." Zoey glared at Khalid as he stood staring at her.

"You are a smart woman. You know you cannot stay here."

"Why ever not?" She hadn't noticed before how short his raven hair was cut, but yet there was a slight wave to it. "Because someone broke into a room?"

"Your room."

"He was probably looking for quick cash or something." Zoey had been rattled at first, but now she was coming to terms with what had happened. "He wasn't quiet. He should have known breaking the glass would wake me."

"It wouldn't most people."

"I'm a light sleeper." She pushed at his chest, and he fell back a step. Her duffel bag had been zipped shut and set by the door. She went to the bed and retrieved her backpack from where she'd hidden it between the nightstand and the bed.

"You hid your backpack?"

"Yes. You don't travel like I do and not pick up a trick or two." She placed her folded shorts inside the front pocket, then faced him. "I don't need to move hotels."

He opened his mouth, but Ryan walked into the room with Babak. Ryan held a plastic sheet, nails, and a hammer. Babak had a broom and dustpan.

Khalid cupped her elbow and reached for her backpack. "You are coming with me. I'm putting you into protective custody."

"What? Oh, no, you're not." She dug her heels in and pulled against his hold. "I have no idea who you are. What gives you that kind of authority?"

His chest puffed up, and a gleam filled his dark eyes. Zoey kept her chin up and held her ground.

"Miss Lacey, I'm afraid I agree," Ryan said. "It's very odd that this happened, especially on your first night here."

"It doesn't make sense." Zoey shook her head. "Look, I can go to another hotel if necessary, which I don't think it is. But I don't need protective custody."

"What if someone else tries to break in?" Khalid tightened his hand on her elbow.

"Who says someone will?" Khalid's protectiveness rubbed her last nerve. She'd had enough of being protected as a child. As an adult she chose her own path.

"I'm not willing to take the chance."

"Well, I am." She yanked her arm away from him.

"You will not." Khalid's voice rose, and Zoey shivered at the steel behind it. "Babak, if you would forgive us for arguing."

"It is fine." He waved his hands. "Let us clean up this mess."

Khalid was overreacting just like her parents used to. Zoey tapped her foot against the floor as Babak cleaned up the glass, and Ryan and Khalid nailed up the sheet of plastic. When they were done, Babak left.

"I'm not arguing with you. I am refusing to go with you." Zoey crossed her arms over her chest.

"You have no choice. If need be, I can make sure it comes from the king himself. A royal decree."

Zoey's mouth dropped open. "You're threatening me." How dare he? She'd done a little research on the royal family. King Malik had recently married a British woman after taking over the throne from his father, who had stepped down after becoming ill. King Malik was a progressive king, but that didn't mean he would be on her side.

"I'm giving you a promise." Khalid leaned down. "I mean it, Zoey. If I have to use royal connections to protect you, I will."

Damn overprotective male. He was backing her into a corner, and she didn't like it. She looked over at Ryan. He'd be no help. Khalid employed him. Her nerves danced at being so close to Khalid. What a heck of a time for her body to realize she was a woman.

"Fine. I'll go with you. For today only." What choice did she have? If she kept refusing, she had a suspicion Khalid would pick her up and carry her out. It would only be for the day.

Khalid blinked and a grin played at his lips.

"Don't look so satisfied." She adjusted her backpack bag. "One day of protective custody. That's it."

Ryan let out a chuckle, and Khalid whipped his head around as Ryan started coughing, but Zoey grinned. It was apparent to her that Khalid wasn't used to being defied. Well, if he hung around her for any length of time, he'd learn.

"I will accept that," he leaned down and whispered in her ear, "for now."

An hour later, Zoey wondered what she'd agreed to. Ryan had left and returned with a big black SUV, into which Khalid piled her and her luggage, and they left Bashir City. Any other time Zoey might have enjoyed the ride, but with Khalid seated next to her, she was distracted.

She wondered who he was, exactly. The local police deferred to him, as did Ryan and Babak. When he'd threatened to call the king, she'd had no choice but to back down. You don't defy the royal family in any country.

The sun was just rising when they arrived at a large, ornate gate, and Zoey cursed herself for being lost in her own thoughts. She knew better, and now she didn't know where she was. The guards at the gate wore uniforms of red and gold. They waved the SUV through, and it immediately turned right, but not before Zoey caught a glimpse of an ornate building.

"Why are we at the palace?" she asked, her fingers tangling in her lap. Oh, brother. Was he going to bring her before the king anyway?

"Here you will be safe," Khalid said as the SUV pulled to a stop in front of a set of bungalows. Khalid hopped out, then opened her door for her.

Zoey started to slip out of the vehicle, but then Khalid's hands framed her waist and he lifted her down. Tendrils of heat swept through her veins. Stop it, she ordered herself. This man is keeping you captive ... well, sort of.

He led her to the bungalow and opened the door, gesturing her to precede him. Zoey stepped into the cool interior. She blinked. This wasn't an ordinary bungalow. The main room was bigger than a small apartment. A soft beige sofa faced a fireplace that had a big screen TV mounted above it, and there were two overstuffed chairs.

Off to her left was a small, fully equipped kitchen. There was a set of stairs that led up to what she assumed was a loft bedroom. The place was warm and inviting.

"Bedroom upstairs, along with a full master bathroom," Khalid said. "Downstairs, living room, kitchen, and bathroom. Full satellite TV and internet. I'll call someone to come stock the kitchen if you give a list of your favorite foods."

"I'm only here for today." She waved her hand.

"We shall see."

Ryan entered with her bags before she could answer. "I'll just put these in the bedroom. And Khalid, we have a meeting shortly."

Khalid nodded. "I'll send someone down with some breakfast if that is acceptable."

Zoey nodded. "My baklava." She'd left it in the hotel.

"I have it, Lady Zoey," Ryan said, holding the white box as he descended the stairs. "I'll put it in the kitchen."

"Thank you, Ryan." Zoey gave him a smile.

"So, you smile at him and not me?"

"Ryan didn't extort me into coming here."

Khalid laughed. "How else was I supposed to get your attention?" He ran his finger over her cheek, and her breath caught in her throat. Ryan stepped out of the kitchen, and Khalid backed away. "Habib will be on duty outside the bungalow."

"Making sure I don't run away?" Why did this man intrigue her so? Make her nerves dance with excitement?

"Making sure you are safe." He brushed his fingers down her cheek once again. "I will return later." With that he turned and left the room, closing the door behind him.

The air whooshed out of Zoey's lungs. Wow. That man was doing a serious number on her libido. Not that she was a virgin or anything, but it had been a while since she'd been with anyone.

She found the remote to the TV and turned it on to local news before running up the stairs and grabbing her camera and laptop. She wanted to look at those photos she'd taken yesterday. She opened her laptop, hoping to dismiss Khalid from her mind, and got to work.

An hour later, Zoey was going through the images on her laptop when someone knocked on the door. She got up to answer it. A young woman stood there with a basket in her hand.

"Lady Zoey, I am Rana. May I come in?"

Zoey stepped back and gestured for the woman to enter. The delicious scent of fresh bread wafted from beneath the cloth cover, making Zoey's stomach growl.

"Sorry I am late," Rana said as she set the basket on the small table next to the kitchen.

"I totally forgot anyone was bringing breakfast," Zoey said, watching Rana pull bread, cheese, fruit, a carafe of fruit juice, and a big container out of the basket. There was also another, smaller container. Zoey went into the kitchen and found plates, utensils, and glasses. "It smells wonderful." She set the table.

"Oh, Lady Zoey, I will not be joining you."

"It's just Zoey." She looked at all the food. "This is all for me?" Zoey shook her head. She might be hungry, but there was no way she could eat all this.

"Yes. The big container has eggs, potatoes, bacon, and sausage. It will easily reheat in the microwave. I will leave so you may eat. If you need anything ask your security, and they will call me." With that, Rana left.

Zoey shook her head, but sat down and opened the big container. The smell of bacon tickled her senses. She dished up a plate and then grabbed a piece of flatbread.

The eggs were fluffy, bacon crisp, the potatoes were seasoned with a spice she couldn't identify, and the bread melted in her mouth. Within minutes she'd polished off her meal. Carefully wrapping up the leftovers, Zoey put them into the fridge and then opened the small container.

There were small round cookies. She took one and popped it into her mouth. Butter and vanilla burst upon her tongue as the cookie practically melted. Zoey closed her eyes and let out a groan. She took two more cookies out of the container before sealing it and putting it in the kitchen.

If she ate too many of those, she'd gain several pounds. With her stomach full, she grew sleepy. Grabbing her laptop and camera, Zoey climbed the stairs to the bedroom.

She cleaned up and changed, then crawled between the covers.

The mattress curved to her body when she turned over. A small grin played over her face. So much better than a too hard or too soft hotel bed. Her lashes drifted shut. A short nap would refresh her.

Khalid strode up to Habib. "How is everything?"

"Quiet. Rana delivered breakfast and left. Nothing since."

"Good. Syed will be here in five minutes to relieve you. Go get some rest."

Habib nodded. Khalid looked up. He could picture Zoey curled up in the bed. Was she wearing the shorts and tank top? His dick jumped, and Khalid shook his head. He didn't have time for a woman in his life.

His need right now was to figure out why someone had been in her room and keep her safe. That was it. Now, if he could just convince his libido. His phone rang. "Yes, okay, I'll be right there." Another small incident in town, but it needed his attention.

Khalid woke with a start, then stood and stretched. Yesterday had been an early and busy day. He glanced at the clock. Five. He'd slept six hours; that was the longest he'd slept at once in a while.

He hadn't purposely avoided Zoey yesterday. There had been a series of little incidents in the city, forcing him and his team to spend all day and some of the night investigating. He'd deal with her anger at having to spend the night later. He and his team were trying to figure out what Kalif was up to. Yesterday he'd read the police report on the man who broke into Zoey's hotel room, all while trying to keep his mind off her. Khalid shook his head. Like that had worked. All he could see was her creamy skin in those shorts and tank top, wondering how she'd look in nothing at all. The woman had gotten under his skin, and he couldn't seem to get her out. Probably because he didn't want to.

He made his way down to the family dining room to get coffee and a bite to eat before he found Rana. He instructed her to take breakfast to Zoey around eight before he made his way back to his office. Ryan would arrive at any moment, and they could go over what they knew and what they didn't. Unfortunately, Khalid had a feeling they knew less than what they needed.

"Good morning, Khalid," Ryan said, walking into his office with a mug of coffee in his hand.

"Morning. All quiet with Zoey?" He'd fully expected one of the guards to come and get him when he'd returned last night.

"No issues that I'm aware of."

Should he be worried? Probably. But for now, he had other things to deal with. "Good. Let's go over the map."

Almost two hours later, Khalid straightened from his desk. "Then we're agreed. We need to send more people out to the east to do recon?"

"Yes." Ryan drew his hand through his hair. "But it will take time, even by vehicle. We're talking at least a day past the last village. I agree with your suspicions that Kalif's base has to be close to the mountains in the east."

"Talk with the men and figure out who is the best to send out."

Khalid rolled the map back up and set it aside. While Kalif's base might be in the east, he had his men everywhere. That thought brought Khalid back to Zoey. Why had someone tossed her room?

"Anything more from the local police about the guy we caught in Zoey's room?"

He didn't know for sure if the men following her had been Kalif's men or not. They'd seemed more intent on mischief than anything else until they'd seen him and run. He had followed, but lost them when they'd blended into the crowds of the marketplace. Why come to her room?

"Nothing but the report we both read," Ryan said.

The report hadn't said much. The man was insisting he thought it was his room. He'd been out late and didn't want to wake his girlfriend. Khalid didn't believe one word of the report. The local police were still holding him on break-in charges. This was a mystery he intended to solve.

A knock sounded at his door.

"Come in," he said.

Rana opened the door and stuck her head in. "I've taken Lady Zoey breakfast."

"Is she awake?"

"Yes, Prince Khalid."

"How is her mood this morning?" he asked.

"She seems fine, Your Highness."

"Very well. Thank you, Rana." Khalid rubbed his chin and made his way out of his office and the palace. He'd talk with Zoey and see if she could find any reason why someone was after her. And possibly apologize for keeping her all night. He ignored the way his nerves tingled with anticipation at being in the same room with the fascinating woman.

Zoey sipped her coffee, trying to keep her temper at bay as she went through the photos she'd taken the other day once again. Something tugged at the edge of her brain. She sorted the photos. Marketplace, buildings, and random people.

When Khalid finally showed up, and he would, she would give him a piece of her mind for keeping her here more than just one day. Yes, she could have had one of the guards go find him, but she had a feeling it wouldn't have made a difference. He wouldn't have showed up. He wanted her there, and there she was to stay.

Irritation itched at her skin as, while she sorted the photos, she nibbled at the bacon Rana had brought her with breakfast. The young girl wasn't very talkative, only saying she'd been asked to bring Zoey breakfast, and since Zoey hadn't complained about what she'd brought yesterday, she'd brought the same breakfast today.

There were more eggs, bacon, sausage, flatbread, fruit, and a big carafe of coffee, along with cream and sugar. More food than she could eat, again. She still had leftovers from last night's dinner in the fridge.

A knock on her door had her lifting her head from her photos. Stretching, she stood and went to open the door. Khalid stood there. Zoey's heart sped up. His raven hair was sticking up in places, as if he'd just rolled out of bed, though his eyes were solemn. Eyes she'd dreamed about last night. *Oh, get a hold of yourself. You're mad at him.*

"Good morning," she said, as she stood back and allowed him to enter. She closed the door and leaned against it, all the while losing the battle not to look at his butt encased in tan pants. God, how did this man have such a fine ass? Did he work out?

"Good morning." His husky voice sent shivers dancing along her skin.

"I'm leaving today," she said, walking back to the kitchen table. Her anxiety at being inside was clawing at her stomach. She needed to get outside for a little bit. "Coffee?" She held up the carafe. Why wasn't she yelling at him? Maybe because it wouldn't accomplish anything? She might be angry with him, but getting into a fight wouldn't do anything but make the issue worse. Years of fighting with her parents had taught her that.

"That would be nice."

Zoey grabbed a mug from the kitchen, poured him a cup, and set it down in front of a chair at the table before she took a chair on the opposite side. "So, when can I leave?"

"You can't. I am sorry." He sipped the hot brew, but his gaze stayed on her.

"Why not?" She jumped out of her chair and began pacing; she couldn't help herself. It was that or start yelling at his enforced custody.

"We haven't found out why the man broke into your room yet. You could still be in danger."

Zoey sighed. "I need to do my job." She waved her hand. "There really was no harm done, except to the lamp and maybe his head."

"I was told he had a nice lump."

"He should. So where does this leave me?"

"I've spoken with the police and one of the king's advisors. If you are willing to have a bodyguard, you could be allowed to do your job."

Zoey let out a sigh and opened her mouth, but Khalid held up his hand. "If you can try and see this from my point of view. We don't know why your room was broken into. We don't know if you are a target, or if it's something else. We want to ensure your safety, but we understand you have things to do. A bodyguard would be a compromise."

"Why such measures for me? I'm just a visitor."

Khalid stared at her. "You called me, remember."

"Yes, because the police were making a fuss, and I didn't want to end up in jail. Instead now I'm in another type of jail."

Her mind ran in circles. What if she just left? Would they put her under house arrest more than she was already? Would the king order a declaration, and she'd be right back where she was now? Could they kick her out of the country? What was she going to do? Really, what choice did she have?

"If I accept this bodyguard, am I allowed to go to back to the hotel?" Already her nerves chafed at the idea of a bodyguard. She really didn't have a problem taking care of herself; she'd done it for years.

Khalid shook his head. "When you are not working, you'll stay here, where I can be sure you are safe."

He was ordering her again. The chafing increased, but she tamped it down. She was in a foreign land and, like it or not, Khalid was right. Two incidents had happened and, until she knew why, she did need to be more careful. She didn't have a death wish. So she would let this play out. Another day or two wouldn't hurt, and then he'd see there was nothing to worry about. "I've been going over the photos I took yesterday to see if maybe there was a reason those young men followed me."

"Anything out of the ordinary?"

"Nothing that I see." She took a sip of her coffee. "So the bodyguard, who would it be?" Ryan was a nice guy but he'd stand out. Heck, probably anyone would stand out with her.

"Habib."

Zoey nodded. She'd met the quiet young man last night. He wouldn't interfere with her work. "He's acceptable."

"I ask, for today, that you stay here while everything is set up to keep you safe."

She gritted her teeth. She needed to get out of this cottage for a little while. "Can Habib take me into town to pick up some supplies? I'd planned on doing it yesterday." She traveled pretty light, so she needed to pick up some personal items. Hopefully, she could grab a few more photos and start writing her first article about Bashir this afternoon.

"I will arrange it. In the meantime, if you can think of any reason why someone would break into your room, I'd like to hear it."

Zoey shook her head. "I have no idea." At least nothing concrete yet.

"Tell me what you did the day before yesterday after you got off the plane." Khalid leaned back as if he had all the time in the world.

Zoey sighed and sat down. "I cleared customs, caught a taxi to the hotel."

Khalid frowned. "You left your luggage at the hotel?"

"Yes. I arrived about midday. My room wasn't ready yet, so Babak held my luggage, and I went out to explore."

He nodded. "Where?"

"I took some pictures outside the hotel, mainly of the street and the buildings. Then I walked to the marketplace, and took pictures of the vendors, food, and flowers. Bought and ate an apple, then moved away from the marketplace, taking pictures of different buildings."

"Did you notice anything unusual?"

"No. I loved the mixture of new and old architecture. That's when I noticed the men following me." Even now her heart rate increased. She hadn't been afraid, but nervous. "I put my camera away in case I needed to defend myself, turned the corner, and ran into you."

Khalid nodded. "I lost the men in the marketplace. How long were they following you?"

"Not long. At least, I don't think so." Her fingers trembled when she lifted her coffee cup.

"They made you nervous?"

Zoey set the mug down with a thump. "A little. I'm a woman alone. It's not the first time men have followed me."

"What?"

Zoey winced at the sound of his voice. "Calm down, will ya? I'm fine. I've learned how to take care of myself. You saw evidence of that when my room was broken into."

"I did." He rested his chin on his fingers. "What does your family think about your traveling the world alone?"

Her spine stiffened. "My family is none of your concern." She picked up her plate and carried it into the kitchen, trying to control her ire. Her parents were not a topic she planned to discuss.

"I apologize. You are correct."

Zoey gave Khalid credit. He backed off when he realized he was overstepping his bounds. The chair scraped back against the floor as he stood.

"I will advise Habib about taking you into town. Is leaving in an hour acceptable?"

"That's fine." Zoey kept her back to him, fighting for her control. Nothing good ever came from her losing her temper; she'd learned that from an early age. At least he was allowing her to go into town.

"Zoey," he started after he'd opened the door.

He stopped, his look unfathomable. Her breathing quickened. They were so close together. One little bit of leaning, and she could kiss him. "Yes." She barely got the word out as she was pulled into his gaze.

His eyes darkened. He leaned forward, then, suddenly, backed up, his lips a thin line. He stepped outside. "Never mind." The door closed quietly behind him.

Her shoulders slumped for a moment before she straightened. What the hell was wrong with her? She'd almost kissed him. Was she crazy? She shook her head to clear her thoughts, pushing the need pulsing in her body into its corner to examine later. At least she'd get into town today and pick up a few things.

An hour later, Habib pointed out the sights to Zoey as they drove into Bashir City. He was a nice young man, probably about her age, but his skin was darker and his features rough. He was soft-spoken, but Zoey found he loved history.

When they parked a few blocks from the marketplace, he reminded her that she needed to stay with him. Zoey smiled and told him she would. And off they went.

By the time she was done, she was sure Habib was happy. Zoey had gone through several shops picking up foods and spices, along with a few pieces of clothing and a couple of magazines. She'd also found a bookstore and picked up a couple of books on Bashir history that Habib recommended.

Along the way, she stopped to take pictures. She talked with the vendors, enjoying their smiles when she spoke their language. The people in the marketplace were open and happy to chat. While some gave Habib a strange look, none mentioned her bodyguard.

"I knew women could shop, but not like that," Habib said as they drove back to the bungalow.

Zoey laughed. "I usually know what I want, but I wanted to explore a bit. I hope it wasn't too bad for you."

Habib shook his head. "Where did you learn to speak Arabic?"

"I've spent a lot of time in the Middle East. It made sense to pick up the language."

"What other languages do you speak?"

"How do you know I speak more than one?" Very few people picked up on that.

"The way you speak. You're almost fluent, and that is hard for a non-native."

Zoey laughed. "True enough. I speak Spanish, French, Italian, Arabic, German, and a smattering of Kurdish, Hebrew, Turkish, Japanese, and Korean."

"Wow." Habib grinned. "That is impressive."

"Thanks, I ... " Zoey broke off, realizing she'd been about to talk about the past she wanted to leave buried. The vehicle turned, and today she got a better view of the palace. "Are we stopping at the palace?"

"Ah, no." Habib's cheeks turned red as they drove through the open gates and turned right.

"Why are we on the palace grounds?" She'd suspected this the day before yesterday but to have it confirmed made her nervous. Was she in trouble with the local authorities? With the royal family?

"The bungalows are here." Habib fell silent, and Zoey made a note to talk to Khalid about it tonight. If she even saw him tonight. His abrupt departure earlier still confused her.

Habib escorted her into the bungalow and carried in her purchases over her objections, then he left. Zoey put everything away and pulled out her laptop. She had too many unanswered questions. Within minutes she sat back and stared at the screen. A quick internet search had given her the answers.

Not that she hadn't researched before she came, just not to this level. Khalid was part of the royal family. How had she missed that? Holy crap. She was lusting after a prince. Why hadn't he told her? Maybe he was keeping that information quiet, but she remembered the way he'd cut Babak off at the hotel. Why didn't he want her to know he was part of the royal family? Would it have changed anything? Maybe, or maybe not. Prince or not, though, she didn't like being ordered around.

Zoey stood up and paced. Was she technically a royal prisoner? If so, why? She let out a sigh. Until she talked with Khalid, there wasn't much she could do. Picking up her camera, she extracted the SD card and slid it into her computer. Might as well get today's photos uploaded and start working on her article.

Several hours later, Zoey stood and stretched. The draft of her article was done. She'd read it over and make corrections before she sent it to the editor, and then she'd cut it down for a blog post.

She glanced out the window to see the sun setting low on the horizon. She hadn't even noticed the passing of time. Her stomach rumbled, and she grinned. Her body knew what time it was.

Zoey strode into the kitchen and pulled out leftovers from the previous night. After reheating the stew, she took the steaming bowl, along with bread and a plate of fruit, to the table.

She ate while she scrolled through her social media feeds. She hadn't posted in a few days, and she really needed to update everyone on where she was. Zoey was aware she had some rabid blog fans.

Opening her Twitter feed, she tweeted that she was in the lovely country of Bashir and would be doing updates to her blog shortly. Within minutes, there were replies and likes. Zoey's heart swelled.

It was little things like this that reminded her of part of the reason she had chosen this path. The other part ... Zoey closed her eyes. She loved her parents, she really did, but their overprotectiveness of her as a child had caused a rift she wasn't sure would ever heal.

She could have rebelled, but by the time she was a teenager, rebelling was the last thing on her mind. Instead, she learned languages and photography, all with an eye on the future.

When she was offered a scholarship to college, her parents wanted her to refuse, but she was eighteen, and they couldn't stop her. It was time for her to get out on her own. Luckily, Zoey made good friends and excelled at her studies. It made up for the lack of a relationship with her parents.

Her ability to pick up languages had opened doors for her, and when she'd graduated, a Fortune 500 company had hired her for translations. She'd enjoyed the job and the travel that came with it, but not the politics. Plus her free time in certain countries was very limited, and she really wanted to get out and explore.

During that time, she'd started her blog. She did it for fun, talking about the places she visited and other cultures. Soon, she had a following, which grew quickly when she started including pictures.

One day she'd received an email from a travel magazine asking her if she'd be interested in writing an article on her last destination. After checking in with legal department at her job, she was given permission to write the article.

She'd really enjoyed it, and after a year, between her blog following and the travel articles, she'd quit her corporate job. Oh, they had tried to convince her to stay, but she'd known corporate wasn't the life for her.

That had been two years ago, and she'd never looked back. She'd only seen her parents a handful of times since she'd left home at eighteen. Now that she was twenty-seven, she should probably make more of an effort, but each time she was with them, they tried to wrap her in cotton wool.

She couldn't be the child they wanted her to be. Zoey carried her dishes into the kitchen. She had just finished washing them when a knock sounded at her door. She opened it to see Khalid standing there. Her blood heated, even as her new knowledge ate away at the fragile trust between them.

"Habib said you wanted to talk to me." His voice was calm and even. She hoped she could be as reasonable as he sounded.

"Yes." The sky was filled with orange, pink, and yellow as the sun began its descent. "Can we talk outside? I need some fresh air."

Khalid nodded and gestured for her to precede him. Zoey shut the door, choosing to walk around the little bungalow. The cool air caressed her skin.

When they reached the backside, Zoey turned to Khalid. She took a shaky breath and blurted out. "Why didn't you tell me you were royal?"

K halid stopped in his tracks at Zoey's question. "How did you find that out?" Damn it. He wanted Zoey to think of him as a normal man, not part of the royal family. Plus he was trying to keep that part of his life separate from his security work. Not that it was easy. Most knew him as a prince first, then head of security.

"Internet."

He groaned. "Zoey, my being part of the royal family has nothing to do with why you are here." It all had to do with keeping her safe and exploring this connection he felt to her. A connection he didn't quite understand.

"Why am I here? On palace grounds?" She placed her hands on her hips and stared at him.

Her defiant stance and firm tone captured his admiration. Zoey was no pushover, but then, he didn't want her to be. He'd always enjoyed a challenge, and his dick stood up and demanded attention in response to her actions. This was damn inconvenient. She was technically under his protection, and he wanted to play instead. In a way, he wasn't surprised at his reaction. She stood up to him, and very few people did that. "Because it is the safest place for you."

"Why? You still haven't explained why you feel the need to protect me."

"Someone broke into your room." Didn't she get she was at risk?

"I'm sure I'm not the first person whose room was broken into in Bashir?"

Khalid frowned. "No, but--"

She held up her hand. "There are no buts, Khalid. I don't need to be here."

"You need to be protected." He drew his hand through his hair. Didn't she understand? He couldn't risk her getting hurt, not on his watch. "Someone broke into your hotel room, and if you hadn't woken, they would have ransacked your room or worse."

Her silver eyes flashed at him. "Am I the first tourist or visitor who's experienced a break-in? What makes you think I need protection? Don't you think you're overreacting a bit?"

He disliked he had to keep things from her, but if Kalif was somehow involved, until he had proof, he couldn't say anything. All he could do was keep her safe. She was too calm about all of this. "No." And he wasn't overreacting, at least not in his book.

"There's just no dealing with you, is there?" She waved her hands in the air.

"This is all about your safety." Why did her flashing eyes and defiant tone turn him on so much? He tried to shake the feelings away, but they were firmly lodged in him.

"No, it's about smothering me." She turned away from him and stared at the other bungalows. There were winding paved paths with what looked like solar lights embedded in the ground. Zoey wrapped her arms around her waist. "You don't even know me, and you're trying to wrap me in cotton wool."

Her words cut him to the bone. He wasn't trying to smother her, but yet she felt that way. Why? Hadn't he let Habib take her to the marketplace today? Let her take her photos without interference? His protective instincts were as high with her as they were with his family.

"Zoey." He put his hand on her shoulder, and a shudder ran through her body. "We finally got the man who broke into your room to talk." He'd received an update an hour ago. "He's part of a small rebel faction. Their leader is a dangerous man. If he wants to hurt you, he will. It's a risk I will not take." He couldn't let her be hurt.

"What could this 'dangerous man' want with me?" She didn't turn to face him, but she didn't pull away from his touch either. "You're not making any sense."

"They take women against their will." Although they had curtailed Kalif's kidnappings and forced labor, that was still a possibility. An icy shiver went up his spine, thinking about what might have happened with Zoey.

"You don't know that's why he broke in. And besides, I took care of him. I've told you I can protect myself."

"You've said that before, but—"

Zoey's elbow slammed into his stomach. The air whooshed out of his lungs as she twisted away from him.

"I'm not helpless." She stomped around him and to the front of the bungalow. A second later, the front door slammed.

He let her go, as this was temporary. She wasn't helpless, but he would not let her stay in town until he knew why she'd been targeted. The watch on his wrist buzzed, and Khalid sighed. He needed to get back to the palace and dinner. Maybe he'd come back afterward and talk some sense into Zoey.

Dinner was a lively affair with his family—his brothers and their respective women. He admired them all. They were strong women for strong men.

"So, how is the adoption of Zain going?" he asked his brother Rafi. Rafi had renounced his succession to the throne so he and his fiancée Bobbie could adopt Zain, who'd been both orphaned and burned in a house fire.

"Well, the final paperwork should be ready soon."

"But first we have to get married," Bobbie said.

"And how are those wedding plans going?" Khalid asked.

"Progressing," Bobbie said. "Thanks to Catherine and Sara." She smiled at the two women.

"The people will enjoy another royal wedding," Khalid said, thinking about all he'd need to do to make sure his family was safe during the celebrations.

"Yes. I do have a question for you, brother," Rafi said.

Khalid stared at his brother. "Yes."

"Who is the woman you are keeping in the bungalow?"

All at once the room erupted.

"Woman?" Catherine stared at him.

"Explain, Khalid," Malik said, his voice strong and stern.

Hell, how did Rafi find out about Zoey? Khalid shouldn't be surprised. Rafi had spied on Kalif's men for months without giving himself away to anyone, not even his own brother.

"It's not the way Rafi is making it sound." Khalid clenched his fingers against his thighs. "I am keeping Zoey safe."

"Safe from what?" Hassan asked.

Khalid quickly outlined the events leading up to Zoey ending up here, including the men following her and the man who had broken into her room. Was it just the day before yesterday he'd brought her here? He felt like he'd known Zoey for much longer. She'd gotten under his skin. Even now his blood heated at the thought of being near her again, even if she was mad at him.

"Well, if that is the case, then bring her to the palace. We have the room," Malik said. "There's more than enough security here to keep her safe."

Malik wasn't wrong. Since Malik had had the palace remodeled, each brother now had his own wing of rooms. He'd made sure all the room were upgraded with bulletproof glass, panic buttons, and reinforced locks. Their parents still had their wing, although they spent more and more time at the summer place in the west.

"That's a perfect idea," Catherine said. "I'm sure she'd be happy to be around other women and not cooped up in the bungalow."

"What is her name?" Sara asked.

"Zoey Lacey." This was getting out of hand, but then his family always had a way of getting what they wanted, no matter how much he protested or tried to protect them.

"That's a pretty name ... wait a second, did you say Zoey Lacey?" Bobbie asked.

Khalid nodded and stared at his soon-to-be sister-in-law.

"Someone you know?" Malik asked.

"Sort of." Bobbie looked at Catherine and then Sara. "We follow her travel blog."

"It can't be," Sara said.

"Khalid, don't tell me you're keeping her from doing her job?" Catherine asked.

He glanced toward the ceiling, willing himself not to react to the censure in Catherine's voice. He respected her more than he could ever say. "I'm trying not to, but she has to be kept safe."

"From what you've said, how do you know she's a target?" Malik asked.

"I don't know if the young men following her were Kalif's or not, but the man who broke into her room was."

"Even you said he didn't have time to do anything, so it could have been random," Rafi said.

Khalid didn't want to agree with his brother. "It is possible, but my gut is telling me it's too coincidental. Her being followed, then the same night her room is broken into."

"Without proof she's in danger," Malik started, "you have a choice. Bring her to the palace or let her go. Otherwise you're going to be dealing with three very irate sisters-in-law."

Khalid glanced around the table and sighed. Damn, his brother was right. All three women were glaring at him. "Very well, but I want it understood, she is not to go anywhere without Habib to guard her."

Everyone nodded, but he didn't miss the glances between the women. He barely prevented himself from rolling his eyes. These women could be a handful. Khalid pushed back from the table. Might as well get Zoey moved tonight, otherwise he'd have no peace. Within minutes he was outside Zoey's bungalow.

"Back for another self-defense lesson?" she asked when she opened the door.

She was still irritated at him. "May I come in?" He tried to ignore the way her light red hair cascaded around her shoulders and her face.

She stepped back and gestured for him to enter. The scent of cinnamon, turmeric, coriander, and onions teased his nose. "Whatever you were brought for dinner tonight smells delicious."

Her shoulders relaxed, and Zoey let out a laugh. "I cooked tonight." She gestured toward the table. "I picked up a few things in town today and made mejadra."

Khalid glanced down at the favorable dish, and his mouth watered. Lentils, rice cooked with cumin, cinnamon, turmeric, and other spices, then topped with crispy fried onions.

"Have you had dinner?" She didn't wait for him to answer. "Sit down and have some. I made way too much for one person." She pulled another plate out and set it on the table for him.

"You are very kind to feed me." He waited until she was seated and then took his seat. While he'd just had dinner with his family, he hadn't eaten much. His first bite of the food had him closing his eyes in bliss. "Where did you learn to make this?"

Zoey grinned, and he noticed her eyes dancing with pleasure. What else would make those silver eyes light up?

"About a year ago, a villager in Turkey taught me. I love the combination of spices and how savory it is. I did add chicken to this one for some protein."

"It is delicious." This woman had hidden depths to her. Why did that surprise him? Zoey was different from most women he knew.

"So to what do I owe the pleasure of your visiting me tonight?"

The word 'pleasure' bounced around in his brain. He wanted to pleasure her all right, first with a kiss, then a caress, then ... he shook his head. Keep your mind on the business at hand, not her delectable body, he told himself.

"Apparently you were discovered today by my brother, Rafi. A discussion happened over dinner, and it was determined you should move into the palace." He didn't say his older brother and king had demanded it.

"Discovered?" Zoey frowned. "Move into the palace? Is that really necessary?"

"It is, unless you want my three sisters-in-law down here invading your space every waking hour of the day." He kept his voice light. He loved the women in his brothers' lives, but they lived life their own ways. Which drove him crazy, making sure everyone was safe.

"Sisters-in-law, huh." A grin played around her lips. "Somehow I don't see you being browbeaten by them."

"You have no idea." He grinned.

"Still, is that a good idea?"

"Probably not, as I'm sure Catherine, Sara, and Bobbie will get you into all sorts of trouble, but you'll be safe there."

"I still don't—" A set of knocks on the front door stopped her words.

Khalid sighed. He stood and then opened the door. "Too late," he threw the comment over his shoulder as three women pushed by him and into the cottage.

"There she is," Catherine said, striding over to Zoey, who had stood.

Zoey's eyes grew wide. "Ummm ... Princess ... I mean, Queen Catherine." Zoey curtseyed.

"None of that." Catherine waved her hand, and Khalid had to hide a laugh. While Catherine was very down-to-earth, she had that royal wave perfected.

Bobbie walked up and pulled Zoey into a hug. "It's great to see a fellow American. I'm a big fan of your blog, by the way."

Zoey let out a laugh, and Khalid relaxed. Zoey could hold her own with the females of his family. That shouldn't have surprised him. Look how well she handled him.

"May I ask what you are doing here?" Zoey asked.

"We've come to help you move into the palace," Sara said. "We've made sure a room is ready for you." Sara winked at Khalid.

His body froze at that wink. What had they done now? His stomach turned over.

"And since Khalid was taking so long we decided to come help," Catherine said, throwing a glance over her shoulder at him.

"We were discussing the move when you three showed up," Khalid said.

"What is there to discuss?" Catherine looked down at the kitchen table. "That smells delicious, what is it?"

"Mejadra," Zoey said.

"I'll have to ask cook to make us some," Catherine said.

"I made it," Zoey said quietly.

Jaws dropped open, and Khalid had to keep from laughing out loud. He loved these women, but not one of them would dare invade the kitchen in the palace.

"You made this?" Bobbie asked.

"Yes. I do a lot of traveling and have been taught a thing or two."

"You are definitely coming up to the palace now," Catherine linked her arm with Zoey's. "Let us help you pack."

Zoey looked at him, and he shrugged. "I'll clean up down here while you go pack."

"There isn't much," Zoey said, as the women led her up the stairs to the bedroom.

An hour later, Zoey marveled at her new room. If she'd thought the bungalow was fancy, this was the lap of luxury. Her room had a huge sitting room, complete with sofa and chairs. There was a small table for two by the window. A bar was complete with coffee and tea service, and there was a small fridge for snacks.

The bedroom was almost as big as the sitting room. A big king-sized bed, covered with what looked like a handwoven quilt, and the bathroom? Okay, she'd died and gone to heaven. Not only did the bathroom have a walk-in shower, but there were also a large garden tub and a closet so large she felt guilty about her meager clothing.

A smile played around her lips. Catherine, Sara, and Bobbie were sweet women, but little firecrackers as well. They'd talked to her nonstop while she packed. Apparently the women weren't just being polite, but were true fans of her travel blog and wanted to hear about how she'd started it and why she kept doing it.

Zoey hadn't had this kind of female companionship since college, and it felt good. She turned, walked over to the balcony doors, and opened them. The warm evening air blew the curtains as she stepped outside.

The smells of jasmine, rose, and ... she couldn't quite figure out the last fragrance that teased her senses as she looked out into the vast garden. Her fingers itched to grab her camera. Tomorrow, in the daylight, she promised herself, as she stared at the flowers and trees.

"I'm not sure it's safe for you to be out here."

Zoey turned to see Khalid striding toward her on the balcony. "Why not?" Why were her nerves dancing at seeing him again? This man was dangerous to her self-preservation.

"Someone could be watching from a distance."

"And I could get hit by a bus tomorrow." She turned back to the garden. "I really think you're overreacting." He took security way too seriously.

"Maybe, but it's my job."

"To annoy people?" She hid a smile as she said the words.

A grin played around his lips. "To keep them safe."

Safe? Zoey didn't want to argue with him anymore. Heck, just being around Khalid would never be safe ... for her heart and her libido. "Why don't we agree to disagree?"

Khalid stepped closer, and Zoey's heart sped up. This man could disarm her so easily. It wasn't like her to react to a man like this. Over-protective men didn't have a place in her life.

"We could." He ran his fingers over her cheeks. "But what fun would that be?"

Fire filled her veins from his touch. She wanted ... no, she needed ... more. Without thought she lifted her hand and curved it around his neck. It didn't take much for her to tug him down and touch his lips to hers. One taste and that was it.

Rich, masculine flavor burst upon her taste buds at the first brush of his tongue against hers, then his arms encircled her waist, and he drew her to him.

Hot tendrils of desire wound themselves around her as he took over the kiss, parting her lips with his tongue. The second her tongue began to duel with his, Zoey knew she was lost.

This man disarmed her like no other, and while she chafed at his control and his need to protect her, she chose to allow herself this moment. To quench the need coursing through her veins, and soul.

5

Khalid hid his surprise when Zoey tugged him down and brushed her lips against his. At the soft feel of her mouth against his, he lost the battle with his own need. Her tender touch melted all his defenses. He slipped his arms around her waist and drew her close as he deepened the kiss.

She tasted of cinnamon and spice, and Khalid couldn't get enough. His tongue dueled with hers as he explored her mouth. Her fingers caressed his neck and for the first time, he wished he had longer hair so he could feel her fingers tangle into it.

Zoey pressed her body against his, raising the temperature in the room. His blood roared through his veins as their kiss continued.

His cock pulsed as their lips parted. Khalid trailed his mouth over her cheek, to her ear, nibbling at the lobe. "You are so responsive."

"I ... " Her voice was soft and breathless.

"I've wanted to kiss you since you first ran into me." The words flowed, and he found they were true. He'd been dying to taste her sweetness.

"It was like running into a brick wall." Her voice was filled with laughter. She leaned back. "What are we doing, Khalid?"

"Kissing, enjoying each other." And he wanted to do more. But first they needed to get off the balcony.

"But this can't go anywhere." She pushed against his shoulders, and he took a reluctant step back. "I couldn't resist tasting you."

""What are you trying to say?" He was curious why she felt their attraction couldn't go anywhere.

"I'm only here for a short time. Once Bashir's anniversary party is over, I'll be on to the next place. The next story."

Khalid frowned. He didn't want to think about her leaving, not now anyway. "We'll—"

An explosion reached their ears, and Zoey clung to him as the ground shook. "Behind you," she whispered.

He turned to see smoke rising from the east. The twilight sky was awash in colors. "Get inside." He pushed her into her room, then dropped a quick, hard kiss on her lips before he turned and ran.

Ryan and his security force waited in front of the palace with an SUV idling. Khalid jumped in, and they took off. "Report?"

"Preliminary, the explosion was outside the city limits," Ryan said, listening to the radio transmission. "No causalities that anyone can see."

Khalid nodded as he pulled on his body armor. After the explosion that had happened in the marketplace, and other small ones, he'd taken precautions for himself and his men.

His cell rang. He looked at the screen. Malik. "Don't know much yet," he told the king. "Explosions outside city limits. Will call you when I know more." He disconnected the call before his brother could get a word in.

They arrived at the affected area within ten minutes. People were milling around. Khalid and his men jumped out and began their search for anyone hurt and for evidence to help them capture those who'd done this.

Zoey stood frozen for a minute after Khalid left, then she grabbed her camera before going back out on the balcony and taking several pictures. Even from this distance she could still see the dust and dirt in the air.

She hoped no one was injured or killed. "Lady Zoey," Habib said as he walked out the balcony doors from the room next to hers. "You should be inside."

"I'm fine." She waved her hand. "Why are you here?"

"My job is to protect you. Khalid ordered it."

Zoey sighed. "What happened?"

"If you please." He gestured for her to move inside. Zoey walked into her room, then turned to Habib when he followed her. "An explosion. I don't know more than that."

"Who would know?" A knock sounded on her door, and she opened it to see a concerned Bobbie standing there.

"Oh, good, Zoey." Then she saw Habib behind her. "I see Khalid wasted no time with your protection."

"Do you know what happened?"

"Come downstairs with me, and maybe we can find out. I know Malik is already on the phone with Khalid and others."

"I have my orders," Habib said.

Zoey started to say something, but Habib motioned her to go, and she followed Bobbie down the stairs and hallway and into a big room. Catherine and Sara were there, with three other men. Zoey made an educated guess these were Khalid's brothers, and the women's husbands or fiancés.

"You've had one heck of a welcome to our country." A man with bright blue eyes crossed the room to them. "I'm Hassan." He held out his hand.

"Zoey."

"Yes, Khalid's guest. I must say, he has good taste."

Zoey's cheeks grew warm.

"I see my soon-to-be husband is flirting. Behave yourself," Sara said, coming up to them.

"I am behaving." Hassan dropped a kiss on top of Sara's head.

"I'm Rafi," the man to her left said. She looked him over and noticed the resemblance to Khalid. "I'm usually the one who charms the women."

"Control yourself," Bobbie said, swatting his arm.

Zoey felt the love. "Any news?"

Hassan turned and gestured to the dark-haired man pacing while talking on a cell phone. Catherine stood next to the desk. "Malik is getting an update now."

Just then the man swore and hung up. Catherine reached out and touched his cheek. His eyes closed, then opened to gaze at her. "Excuse my language." He crossed the room to the group, bowing his head slightly. "Malik, the one in charge. I hope Khalid has been taking good care of you."

"He's been very kind, even if I don't think I need protection."

Malik laughed. "Sounds like him. Come sit down, and I'll brief everyone." Over the next ten minutes she learned that four small explosions had all gone off at the same time. No one was hurt, just a lot of dust and dirt, and they were still searching to see if there were any more devices.

"We're not usually a war-torn country," Rafi said.

Zoey shook her head. "I realize that this is unusual. I did do some research on Bashir before I came."

"Bobbie mentioned you were in Iraq?" Rafi said.

"Yes. I was doing a set of articles on some of the smaller villages."

"How bad is it there?" Malik asked.

"Bad, but the people are strong. I did a five-part story about Iraq and what I saw. It should be coming out shortly."

"Wait, I thought you just did travel pieces," Hassan said.

"Usually, but while I was Iraq I was approached by a worldwide magazine asking if I was interested in writing about the people of Iraq and how the war affected them. Since I was there, I figured why not. And the money helped finance my trip to Bashir."

"Why Bashir?" Sara asked.

"I'd heard about the wedding celebration; I even watched a little bit of it on TV." She didn't mention she thought it was a fairytale come true. "Then I heard about the 300th anniversary and decided it would be fun to cover it." Let alone she wanted to explore this country and understand the people.

"Tell us about your other travels," Malik said.

"Are you sure?" Zoey wasn't used to talking about herself.

"I'm interested. Please, it will keep our minds off of our brother."

Zoey hadn't thought about that. "Is Khalid in danger?" Her stomach clenched. He was always going on about her protection, but what about his? He was part of the royal family, after all. How could they let him put himself in danger?

"Malik." Catherine slapped her hand on his chest. "Khalid will be fine, Zoey. But I'm like my husband. I'd love to hear more about your travels. I love your blog."

"Let's go into the family room and get comfortable," Hassan said.

Zoey followed them down the hall into another big room. This one made her smile. Overstuffed chairs and sofas in browns and beiges.

Zoey sat down as the others did. They looked at her, and she began talking. Maybe it would keep her from worrying about Khalid, but she doubted it.

"Bed, all of you," Khalid told his security force when they returned to the palace grounds after midnight.

His men didn't grumble, which told him just how tired they were. He was tired as well. Almost six hours of shifting through mounds of debris, making sure there were no more devices, and interviewing people in the area. No one had seen anyone in the area who didn't belong.

Thankfully, no one had been hurt. Kalif was grating on his nerves, though. At least this was not as bad as the marketplace bombing a few months ago. Still, bombs at the edge of the city were a reminder Kalif was dangerous and had to be stopped.

The problem was finding the man. Khalid sighed as he made his way toward the sitting room where he knew his family would still be gathered. He would meet with Malik and Ryan officially tomorrow. They could brainstorm ideas of what to do to find and capture Kalif.

Laughter reached his ears as he drew closer to the room. Khalid paused in the doorway. Zoey was speaking, and his family seemed enthralled. He wasn't surprised. She was the most intriguing woman he'd ever been around, and that was saying something based on his sister-in-law and soon to-be sisters-in-law.

Rafi looked up. "Khalid," he said.

Zoey stopped talking, jumped up, and took several steps before she stopped, the worry in her eyes evident. He held open his arms. She ran to him. "You're back. Are you okay?" she asked, throwing her arms around him.

He automatically put his arms around her waist, holding her to him. "I'm fine, just tired." He enjoyed the feel of her body against his. Having her arms around him. Having someone to welcome him home. Not that his family didn't, but with Zoey it was different. He could get used to coming home to her waiting embrace.

"Any injuries?" Hassan asked.

"No, I would have called if there had been." He released Zoey, then guided her over to the chair she'd been sitting in. "We were right, it was all outside the city limits."

"Why? I don't get this," Bobbie said.

"I don't either." Khalid took the chair next to Zoey as she yawned. "Malik, it's late. Everything is stable for now. If you don't mind, Ryan and I will brief you in the morning."

"Do you mind if I join you for that?" Rafi asked.

"You are more than welcome."

"Well, since there are no injuries, and everything seems to be under control, I don't have an issue with waiting until first thing in the morning. I suggest we all get some rest," Malik said, standing. "Is the police department on alert?"

"Yes." Khalid rubbed the back of his neck. His men had wanted to stay in town, but the police were more than capable, and they needed rest.

Khalid escorted Zoey upstairs to his wing as the others called out good night and made their way to their own rooms. Habib stood outside her room.

"Habib, thank you," Khalid said.

Habib nodded his head. "I will stay until morning when I can be relieved."

"Go now. All is well." Habib took his job seriously. Like Khalid did.

"Yes, sir." Habib left, and Zoey looked at him.

"Why was Habib still here? I thought my being here meant I was safe?"

"You are. He was under orders to make sure you stayed safe. While you were with the family, he made sure no one disturbed your room."

"But—"

Khalid placed his fingers against her soft lips. "We've had incidents happen in the palace in the past. The issues have been dealt with, but I refuse to take chances." He pushed open her door and stepped inside. Nothing out of place, balcony doors closed. "Stay here." He checked out the rest of her quarters before returning to her side with a yawn.

"Go get some sleep, Khalid." She brushed a kiss over his cheek. "We can talk more tomorrow."

"We can. Lock the door and rest well." He brushed a kiss over her forehead, then stepped out of the room reluctantly. He waited until she'd closed the door and locked it before he made his way to his room, which was next to hers. He was exhausted and hoped he would sleep. Sleep hadn't come easily to him in a long time.

His brothers complained about burning the candle at both ends, but he'd never told them about the nightmares. He'd never told anyone of the one mistake that still haunted him.

Early the next morning, Zoey scrolled through the photos on her computer once again. She'd already written three more articles and several blog posts. There was something nagging at her about the photos.

She flipped through them again and again, yet she couldn't put her finger on it. Maybe if she could print them and lay them out on a table to figure out what bothered her. A glance at the clock showed her it was only eight. She'd been up since six. She'd fallen asleep around one, but at six she was wide awake.

It wasn't unusual for her. That's why she usually made sure she didn't share a room with anyone. Once she woke up, she could rarely go back to sleep. Pushing her computer aside, Zoey stood, stretched, and went in search of some food. Five minutes later, one of the maids directed her to the dining room, where food was set up.

Zoey grabbed some coffee and filled a plate before sitting down. She had just started to eat when Malik and Catherine walked in. Instantly she stood up.

"Sit down, please. We're not formal." Catherine waved her hand at Zoey.

Zoey sat, but didn't start eating again until Catherine and Malik began eating. "I hope it's okay I'm here. A maid directed me here."

"It's fine," Malik said. "As Catherine said, we're not formal, but I am curious why you're up so early."

Zoey shrugged. "I woke up and couldn't go back to sleep." Just then Khalid walked in, looking more tired than he had the previous night. Her stomach clenched. "Did you sleep at all?" she asked before she could censor herself.

"A bit," he said, as he poured some coffee and got food.

"Does Hassan need to give you something?" Malik asked.

"I'll be fine. Just keyed up after last night," Khalid said.

Malik opened his mouth and then shut it, making Zoey wonder if this was a pattern with Khalid. Not that she needed to pry into his life, but she was well aware of how insomnia could affect a person. If he wasn't rested, he wouldn't be at the top of his game, security-wise. That worried Zoey a lot more than she thought it would.

Zoey waited until Khalid sat next to her. She toyed with the food on her plate. With Khalid this close, her nerves danced with excitement, but she could also see the fatigue lines in his face. She knew what fatigue could do to a person. "Would it be okay for Habib to take me into town today? I saw a photography shop the other day, and I'd like to go get some photos printed."

"Don't you work digitally?" Malik asked.

"Usually, yes, but ... " She glanced up at Khalid and he was watching her. "Something about the pictures I took the other day is nagging me."

"What is it?" Khalid set his fork down.

"I'm not sure. I keep going back to the pictures, thinking I'm missing something."

"You believe printing them out will help you?" Malik asked.

"I hope so. I'm thinking if I can lay them out side-by-side I'll see something."

Malik nodded. "We have printers you can use."

"I appreciate this, but I needed high-quality photo printing."

"Malik and I have a meeting after breakfast, so I'll take in you into town after we're done."

The events of last night rushed back into her mind. "You don't need to take time away from your work. I'm fine going with Habib." Zoey glanced from Khalid to Malik and back. They had more important things than to interrupt their day for her.

"It's fine. I'd rather take you myself. Finish eating."

His tone was firm and no nonsense. Zoey nodded. Not that she was hungry anymore. Instead, she drank her coffee and nibbled at her food until Khalid was done eating.

"Meet me at the front door at eleven," he said, standing.

"Is that enough time for your meeting?" She didn't want him rushing through for her. There could be lives at risk here.

Khalid glanced at Malik, who nodded. "It's fine. See you then." He brushed his fingers down her cheek.

Fire followed his touch. Malik's eyes widened, and a smile touched his face. She kept her gaze on Khalid until he left the room with his brother. Catherine let out a sigh.

"I love those two, but sometimes they take their duties too seriously," Catherine said.

"I don't have enough information about Malik to agree or disagree, but Khalid? Yes, he does take protection very seriously. Do you know why?" That was probably a question she should ask Khalid, but if Catherine could give her some insight into this man who made her blood heat and body throb, then all the better.

"Not really." Catherine shook her head. "He's been this way since I've been here. The al-Hakim men are very intense."

"That I agree with." Zoey finished her coffee and stood up. "I'll see you later." She left the room and jogged up the stairs. She'd already copied the pictures to a flash drive and another SD card. She put them in a special case she used just for them, and slipped it into her backpack.

Since she had some time, she started organizing the other pictures she'd taken. Her mind started buzzing. Would the royal couples allow her to do a story on them? They each had interesting stories on how they'd met and their lives together.

By the time she'd finished sketching out her idea and a way to present it to everyone, it was almost eleven. Slinging her backpack over her shoulder, she made her way back downstairs to the front door, where Khalid already waited for her. "I hate that I'm taking you away from your work."

"It's fine." He ran a finger over her cheek. "Let's go."

Habib was in the front seat of the SUV with a driver. As they pulled through the palace gates, Zoey turned to him. Her nerves danced as she debated what she wanted to say. "Khalid, why don't you take Malik up on his offer to have Hassan prescribe you something to sleep?" She might be overstepping her bounds, but that had never stopped her before.

"It will be fine." He pulled a piece of rope from his pocket.

She stared at the piece of rope. Interesting. Zoey had seen denial before. She had gone through it herself. And she might be overstepping her place, but somehow, Khalid had wiggled his way inside. While she didn't want to examine that too closely, she'd come to care about his welfare. Keeping quiet had never been a strong point for her, so she plunged ahead, covering her hand with his. "We all get insomnia now and again. Hassan can give you something to help you fall asleep. You don't have to do this alone."

His dark gaze rose, and their eyes met. "All is well, Zoey."

"But it's not." She shook her head. "Look, I know I'm the outsider here, but sometimes that allows me to see things. I know the signs, because I've experienced them." If she was going to get through to him, then she had to open up to him.

His eyebrows rose, and he frowned. "Are you not sleeping?" Instantly his demeanor changed.

"Always worried about everyone else," she said, smiling. "When was the last time you've slept more than four hours?" It was guess, but that was usually about how long she'd slept when she was having issues with insomnia.

"Several months." His features froze. "Why did I tell you that?"

"Because I'm probably the first one to ask you point-blank." She rubbed her fingers over the back of his hand.

"I'll be fine, Zoey." He was trying to shut her down, and while she didn't want to let him, she knew when it was time to back off.

"I'm sure you will. But if you don't get some sleep, you won't be able to protect anyone."

Khalid let out a groan, and she hid a smile. She pulled her hand back and watched as Khalid began to knot the rope, creating an intricate pattern with it.

"That's very interesting." Her memory banks fired. The design reminded her of the time she'd spent in Japan. "Shibari?"

His eyes widened. "You know shibari?"

"I spent a week in Japan several years ago and was treated to a demonstration. It is a beautiful art. Even more so when there is a connection between the two people doing it."

He stared at her for a moment before turning his attention back to the rope in his hand. "It is. It helps settle my mind." He pulled the rope apart, then he lifted her hand and cradled it in his lap as he began tying the rope around her fingers and palm. "There is something soothing about doing it."

Zoey sat perfectly still as he created a work of art around her hand. The rope was soft against her skin, and Khalid never pulled the rope tight enough to affect her movement. When he was done, she held up her hand.

She didn't know how to explain it. It was like a fingerless glove with a pattern. "That is fantastic." She wiggled her fingers, enjoying the feel of the rope against her skin.

Khalid smiled, then undid the rope. Regret flashed through her for not getting a picture of his work but also because he removed it. Zoey wondered if he'd ever worked with a live person. And why did it make her hot to think about him tying her up with rope? She enjoyed a little kink in her life, but it had never gone beyond toys or a little spanking. Maybe having her lover hold her hands over her head, but nothing more than that.

The SUV stopped just as Khalid undid the last of the knots. He took her hand, brought it to his lips, and kissed her fingers. "Your skin is so fair, I will need to be careful."

Careful? Was he thinking about tying her up? Her blood heated. She looked at her skin. It was a little pink, but nothing that wouldn't fade in a few minutes. A thrill of excitement went through her at his words. Was she crazy? She was only here for a little while and then would be on to her next job.

That didn't mean she couldn't have a little fun while she was here. Khalid opened the door and helped her out of the SUV. What was she thinking? He was part of the royal family. One didn't just have a fling with royalty.

They walked down the street to the small printing business she'd noticed the other day. Inside, computers were set up for people to print photos. Khalid went and talked with the owner as she sat down and plugged in the flash drive. Within minutes, she had the photos selected and sent for printing.

The sound of voices had her looking at the door. People were crowded there, talking in low tones, watching her. Khalid walked over to the group and motioned them back.

Zoey wondered what was going on. She put the flash drive away, then joined the owner.

"The photos will be ready in just a minute, Lady Zoey," he said.

"Why do you call me Lady Zoey?" She'd noticed that the other day at the palace but had forgotten to ask why.

"It is a sign of respect in our country, especially for one who is part of our royal family."

"I'm not part of the royal family." Where was he getting that idea? Heck, she'd only been in Bashir a few days. Was that all it was? A couple of days? So much had happened, and inside her heart she wouldn't trade those days for anything.

The man just smiled, then turned to get her photos. He gathered them up and put them into an envelope for her. "Here you go, Lady Zoey."

"Thank you. How much do I owe you?"

"Oh, no, all has been taken care of. Go. Enjoy." He waved his hands. Zoey wanted to protest but decided against it. She stepped outside the shop to see Khalid surrounded by people.

Unable to help herself, she pulled out her camera, slid the envelope in her backpack, and started taking pictures. She captured the way the older men stood waiting for their turn, the older women beaming at him, the children clamoring for attention by tugging at his legs.

Her vision blurred for a minute. These people loved and admired him and probably the rest of the royal family too. Zoey turned and took pictures of the street. The marketplace vendors were just setting up, and she was able to get some great pictures. "You are an artist with the camera," Khalid whispered in her ear.

Zoey ducked her head. "I enjoy it." Putting the camera away, she turned to him. "I'm done. Are you?"

He glanced over his shoulder. While the crowd was still there, they no longer surrounded him. "Yes." He cupped her elbow and escorted her back to the SUV.

"Is it like that whenever you go out?" she asked as they drove back to the palace.

"Not always. The people of Bashir are excited about the anniversary, and they were asking question about the parade and such."

"Parade?" She hadn't read much on the anniversary party, something she needed to do.

"Yes. The royal family participates in a parade. It's going to be a security nightmare."

"You worry a lot about your family, don't you?" He worried about everyone. It was too much for one man. She wondered if she'd ever get him to see that. Wait a second, was she thinking long term? No, she had to stop that. Once her job was done, she'd be off again.

"Yes." He let out a sigh. Just then a pop sounded and the SUV wobbled. "Down." He pressed her down sideways against the seat and covered her body with his. A second pop sounded.

Habib was yelling and the driver swearing as the SUV wobbled along. "Help on the way," Habib grunted out as the SUV stopped.

"No one get out. Keep the doors locked." Khalid sat up. "Zoey, stay down."

Zoey's heart pounded in her chest. "What is going on?" It felt like they'd blown a tire.

"Someone shot out the tires." Khalid's head turned as he looked out the back window. "Habib, are you armed?"

"Always, Khalid. So is the driver."

"Are you expecting a shootout?" Zoey trembled. This was very unexpected. Bashir was a safe country from what she read. Even Rafi had said last night this wasn't normal.

"No." Khalid ran his hand down her back. "There's no reason to worry, I will keep you safe."

"I know you will." And she did. But that didn't mean she wasn't frightened. Zoey shifted so she could keep her gaze on Khalid. This was so very different from Iraq, at least to her. While there had been some intense moments with insurgents, this seemed more intense. This was different. This seemed more personal.

In Iraq, she hadn't usually been a target or even in a situation where she could get shot. She'd been in towns where shootings had happened while she was there, but it had never happened to her or right in front of her.

How long before help arrived? Khalid seemed calm as he kept watch. Habib and the driver were silent. How much longer? Her racing heart calmed a bit, but her stomach turned over and over.

Finally, after what seemed to be hours, two SUVs pulled up, and armed men jumped out. Khalid reached for the door.

"Khalid." She grabbed his hand, half sitting up.

"My security forces," he said, giving her hand a squeeze and flashing her a brief smile before opening the door. "Stay here," he said, and the door shut behind him.

Zoey took a breath as she sat up. "All is well, Lady Zoey," Habib said before he got out. Zoey wasn't so sure about everything being well, but at least for now they were safe.

She waited until Khalid finally opened the door and gestured for her to get out. "The area is clear."

"Did they catch whoever did this?" She scanned the area.

"No, but we're still searching. I want you to go back to the palace."

"What? If there's no danger. I can wait while the tire is changed."

"Zoey." His tone became deep and firm.

She put her hands on her hips. "If I go back, you go back."

He shook his head. "Be reasonable."

"Reasonable?" Her anger rose. "Someone shot out the tires on the SUV. They were shooting at you."

"You don't know that. You could have been the target."

"Please." She marched up to him and poked him in the chest. "There's no reason for anyone to shoot at me, but you ... " She poked him again. "You're royal."

"I'm fine."

"And so am I. Get this straight. I'll go back when you go back."

"Stubborn woman. Don't you understand your safety is the most important thing to me?"

"Thank you, but you need to understand I won't leave you behind."

Habib chuckled, and Khalid glared at him before turning his gaze back to her. "Which is why you're not going to like this." He picked her up in his arms and set her in the waiting SUV. "I'll be back at the palace soon."

"You'll ... " She was so angry she couldn't get the words out. Zoey looked down. While he'd talked, he'd somehow used his rope to tie her wrists together, and now they were fastened to the seatbelt he'd put around her.

"Habib will untie you when you arrive at the palace." He slammed the door shut, and the vehicle moved away.

Zoey swore under her breath as she struggled, but he had her expertly tied. Oh, they were going to have a talk about his hero complex when he got back, because she was beyond angry with him.

Malik was standing on the steps of the palace along with Rafi when the SUV pulled up. Habib jumped out of the front seat, opened her door, and untied her hands. "Thank you, Habib," she said. She wouldn't be rude to him. He was just following orders. She snagged her backpack from where it sat on the seat next to her and marched up the steps. "Your brother is a stubborn, bullheaded idiot," she said as she walked past the two brothers.

"I think that describes all of us at one time or another," Rafi commented as they followed her into the palace.

"Well, Khalid takes it to a new level." Zoey stopped at the stairs and turned to the men. "Is there a room with a big table I can use?" She needed to use up some nervous energy.

Malik nodded. He led Zoey down a hallway. "Khalid said you had a flat tire."

"We did have a flat tire, yes. Two of them. Someone shot them out."

"What?" Malik's voice rose. "Someone shot at you?"

"At the vehicle." She stopped and stared at him.

Rafi rubbed his chin. "Khalid failed to mention that. Should I ... "

Malik shook his head, "I'll deal with our uncommunicative brother when he gets back. Are you okay, Zoey?"

"I'm fine." She waved his concern away. "Except I'm more worried about Khalid. What if the shooter comes back?"

"All will be fine," Malik said, giving her shoulder a squeeze. "Here we go, this is a conference room we use for meetings."

Zoey glanced inside the room. Black executive chairs sat around a big, gleaming oak table. The room had dark paneling. It would do.

Rafi walked in and opened the curtains. "Thank you." Zoey placed her backpack on the table. "I'm going to get my laptop and start going over these."

"Do you need anything else?" Malik asked.

Knocking some sense into Khalid would be nice, but ... Zoey shook her head. Hopefully she'd be able to concentrate and not worry about Khalid. But her stomach clenched. She'd just met him and only kissed him once, but her emotions were already involved. He had to be safe. He'd better be safe, or he'd answer to her. Oh, he'd answer anyway, because he wasn't going to get away with wrapping her in cotton wool; she'd had enough of that as a child, and it was time Khalid learned that.

Khalid knelt and picked up the spent shell casing with a glove. Long range. He straightened and looked at Ryan. "Well, whomever it was, they were sloppy in leaving the shell casings behind." Khalid dropped the evidence in the bag Ryan held.

"They were aiming for the tires, not the vehicle," Ryan said.

They'd inspected the vehicle and the only damage was to the tires. A sharpshooter. He felt his level of tension rise. A sharpshooter could be dangerous and unpredictable. He should know.

"All our vehicles are bulletproof, so that makes sense. The question is why?" He kept asking himself that question.

"You could have been the target."

"I've thought of that, but then why didn't they try to attack us after we were disabled?" Khalid rubbed his chin. Nothing made sense right now. Once the SUV had been stopped, it took time for help to arrive. Whether the vehicle was bulletproof or not, they could have swarmed the SUV. His cell rang. "Khalid here."

"You lied to me."

His brother's furious voice caused Khalid to wince. "Not really. We did have a flat tire."

"Khalid." Malik was in full king mode. "I expect a full report when you get back, which will be in the next thirty minutes, or I'll come get you myself."

The line went dead, and Khalid shook his head. Yes, his family worried about him. But he was more worried about them and what Kalif was up to. "I'll let you and the team finish up. I've been ordered back to the palace."

Ryan laughed. "As if you'd listen if you didn't want to."

Khalid shook his head. Ryan was right. He loved his brother, his entire family, but he chose to go back to the palace now rather than to keep investigating. He didn't want to stir the hornets' nest just yet, and he still had Zoey's ruffled feathers to smooth over.

Twenty minutes later, Khalid walked into his brother's office. Malik glared at him. Khalid held his hands up. "I needed to investigate."

"I understand, but next time tell me the truth. When Zoey mentioned being shot at, I thought the worst." Malik gestured to the chair. "So, tell me what happened."

Khalid explained about the tires being shot out, his sending Zoey back to the palace, and what he'd found before he was ordered to return.

"Do you think this has anything to do with the explosions yesterday?" Malik frowned.

He was worried, and Khalid didn't blame him. "Nothing points to Kalif, but who else would do something like that?"

"I've been communicating with the tribal leaders. Since they denounced Kalif, he hasn't bothered them."

"That is good. The tribal leaders are still supporting you, right?" There had been some issues with them in the beginning, but Khalid was sure his brother had finally won them over.

"Yes. They are beginning to understand that while I encourage their teaching the old way of life, we have to move forward. If we stay in the past, our country will die out. No one wants that."

"No, we don't. Where is Zoey?" He'd half-expected her to be waiting to pounce on him the second he walked in. He rubbed his hand over his face, trying to think of how he was going to deal with her.

A gleam flashed in Malik's eyes. "Conference room, going over the photos." Malik stood, and Khalid followed suit.

At least she was working. That was probably a good thing for him. "I'm going to go check on her, then I'll be in my office." Khalid strode out of Malik's office and straight to the conference room. Zoey stood there rearranging the photos on the table, then moving them again. "Anything?"

Her head lifted from her task. "Khalid." She maneuvered around the table and threw her arms around him. "Everything okay? Are you all right?"

He closed his arms around her, enjoying the feel of her body against his, especially in a surprise hug. "I'm fine." She was worried about him, and his heart swelled. Why did this feel different than Catherine being worried about him? Or his brothers? Or Sara and Bobbie?

"Good." She stepped back and punched him on the arm.

"Hey." His eyes widened. Damn, this woman had a good punch. No one but his brothers had ever hit him, and that had been in fun when they were children.

"Don't ever do that to me again. Never send me home when you could be in danger. And you lied to your brother about it." She stomped around the table and back to him. "I've been worried sick, and I'm so angry with you." She threw her hands in the air.

"Would it help if I said I'm sorry?" He fought against grinning. She was magnificent when she was angry.

"No." She glared at him. "You tied me up."

The hurt in her eyes almost broke him. "I couldn't protect you and investigate at the same time."

Her eyes turned glacial. "Get out of here and let me work." She turned back to her photographs.

Khalid rubbed the spot where she'd hit him, but a grin played around his lips. She cared. Otherwise why would she be so upset? "I'll be in my office, it's just down the hall on your left. If you need anything, let me know."

"Go." She waved her hand at him. He was tempted to stay and see what she'd do, but instead he shook his head and left her to her work. Later would be soon enough to discover more of the fire beneath her calm surface.

~

Zoey breathed out a sigh of relief when Khalid left the conference room. She was angry, but she was also happy he was safe. She wanted to hold him the rest of the day and keep him from harm, but that wasn't realistic. Realistic or not, her heart begged her to go after him, but her head fought back. She didn't need a man to complete her life, and she had work to do.

Pushing all thoughts of Khalid away, she turned her attention back to the photos and began rearranging them once again. There it was. Snagging one of the executive office chairs with her foot, she sat down, then pulled up the same images on her computer and enlarged them.

The series of photos showed the men who'd followed her. They'd been by the intriguing design she'd taken a picture of. She pulled up the design and stared at it.

It didn't have a meaning to her. It was just a beautiful design, but that didn't mean it didn't mean something to the Bashirian people. She looked up as Ryan was walking past the conference room.

"Ryan, are you on your way to see Khalid?"

"Yes."

"Good. Would you please ask him to come in here and have him ask Malik as well? I think I've found something."

Ryan's eyes lit up. "Wonderful, give us a few minutes."

Zoey put away the photos she didn't need and then arranged the other ones in the order they needed to be in. She'd just finished up when Khalid, Malik, and Ryan walked in.

"Ryan said you had something," Khalid said.

"Yes. And I'm hoping one of you knows what it means." She motioned them over to her. She showed them the photos, one by one, then showed them the design. "I think this is why they were following me. Because I took a picture of it."

Malik straightened. "I've seen that before."

"Me too." Khalid stared at the wall. "I just can't remember where. Ryan?"

"Nothing."

"Hey, what's going on?" Rafi asked as he and Bobbie entered the conference room.

"Rafi, come look at this. Khalid and I have seen it but can't remember where," Malik said, waving his brother over.

Khalid moved out of the way so his brother could look at the picture. "Where did you get that?"

"You recognize it?" Zoey asked.

"Yes, it's an old design. It signifies a call for peace," Rafi said.

"That's it." Khalid rubbed his forehead. "We found markings like that around the marketplace a while back, not as big."

"Yes," Rafi said. "I was talking with the tribal leaders, and they showed it to me in the old records."

"Zoey, where did you take this?" Malik asked.

"About a block before the building Khalid was using for his security team."

"Maybe that's why the men followed you and why we were shot at," Khalid said.

"Why would you think that?" Zoey stared at him.

"You were in the vehicle and had just printed those photos."

"Yes, but there's no way anyone could know that. Only the owner knew what I printed out."

"Malik shook his head. "I don't believe the owner would be involved."

"Malik, we have to suspect everyone," Khalid said.

"But if the symbol means peace, why would someone be upset I took a picture of it and attack us?" Zoey asked.

"I don't know." Malik rubbed his chin. "Rafi, would you talk to the tribal leaders and maybe with a couple of the scholars at the university and see if this symbol means anything else and why someone would want to protect it?"

"Sure. It all could be a coincidence," Rafi said, picking up the photo. "Is it okay if I take this, Zoey?"

Zoey nodded.

"I really don't believe in coincidences," Khalid muttered.

She shook her head. "You suspect everything. In the meantime," Zoey began gathering up the photos, after making sure Rafi had what he needed, "I need to get out there and do my job."

"And that's our clue to get lost," Rafi said, chuckling.

Zoey laughed as everyone but Khalid filed out of the room. He opened his mouth but Zoey held her hand up.

"I know you want to keep me safe, but I do have a job. I'll take Habib with me." Khalid crossed his arms over his chest.

"Oh, excuse me," Bobbie said when she walked into the room. "I was told Rafi was in here."

"He was. He's probably in Malik's office. Is everything all right?" Khalid asked.

"Fine. We're due at the hospital with Zain for his appointment," Bobbie said.

"Is that where Catherine's mural is?" Zoey asked.

"Yes," Bobbie said. "If you want to come with us, you're welcome to."

Zoey looked at Khalid.

"All right, but Habib stays with you."

"Thank you." She kissed his cheek. "Can you give me five minutes to grab my stuff?"

"Sure. I need to go find my soon-to-be-husband anyway. Meet you by the front door." Bobbie turned and left.

Zoey sat back in the SUV as they left the hospital several hours later. Zain dozed between Rafi and Bobbie.

"Is he doing all right?" Zoey asked. The little boy was cute but still a bit shy around her.

"Tired. That's the last of the doctor visits for a while, thank goodness," Bobbie said, brushing a long strand of hair from Zain's forehead.

"How did you like the mural?" Rafi asked.

"It's beautiful. Catherine did a fantastic job." Zoey had taken picture after picture. "Rafi, do you think Catherine would mind if I interviewed her?"

"You're part of the family. I don't see why she would mind."

"Part of the family?" Now she was really confused.

Bobbie grinned. "A part of our extended family." Bobbie glanced at Rafi and then back to Zoey. "What did you have in mind?"

Zoey wasn't sure how she felt about being called part of the royal family, even as an extended member. It wasn't like she and Khalid were dating or anything. And she was only in the country for a short time. She wouldn't correct Bobbie now, but later she'd ask what this was all about.

"Well, I'm thinking about a small art magazine that's always looking for articles on artists. I bet they'd be interested in Catherine's work, and it would have human interest since she's now queen."

Her idea from earlier took a hold in her mind. What fun it would be to interview not only Catherine, but all the women. How they came to Bashir and fell in love. There were several magazines that would eat that up.

"I'm sure Catherine will be fine with it," Bobbie said.

"Actually, I'd like to interview all of you."

"All of us?" Bobbie's voice rose.

"Only if you want." Zoey saw how Bobbie reacted to her words. She wondered if there was a story there. "It doesn't have to be anything formal."

"I think that's an excellent idea," Rafi said, hugging his soon-to-be wife. "It would be great PR for Bashir."

"I'll have to think about it," Bobbie said, as the vehicle pulled up to the palace.

Zoey slipped out of the vehicle. "Take your time, Bobbie. I'm going to go find Catherine and Sara and see what they think."

7

Khalid pushed aside the report he was reading. It was almost six. Rafi and Bobbie should be back from the hospital by now. So where was Zoey? And why did he expect her to show up in his office? Did she even know where it was?

It wasn't like him to be so tied up about a woman. He looked at the piece of rope in his hand. He'd been playing with it for the last hour as he read. He wondered if Zoey would let him tie her up like she had him tied up.

She hadn't resisted on the way to the city this morning when he'd tied her hand. She'd mentioned how decorative she found it. That's what shibari was for him. Decorative. It could lead to some intense sex. The concentration it took for him to create the knots centered him, and with the right person, it could led to a very deep emotional connection, though he'd never yet tried that.

He pushed away from his desk, tossed the piece of rope down, and headed out. Rafi was in the entryway with Zain in his arms.

"Where are the women?"

"They're in the lounge talking. I'm going to take Zain up to his room. He woke up long enough to eat a snack but fell right back asleep." Rafi climbed the stairs toward his wing.

Khalid turned and made his way to the lounge. He heard laughter before he even reached the room. It warmed his heart to see Zoey getting along so well with the others. She fit right in.

"How was your afternoon?" Khalid asked as he entered the room.

"Great. Catherine is a very talented artist."

"She is."

"Please, enough," Catherine waved her hand. "Zoey, I'll make time on my schedule for you."

"Me too," Sara said.

Then they looked at Bobbie, who squirmed in her seat. "Oh, all right."

Khalid wondered what was going on.

"Great, thank you all." Zoey picked up her camera. "And don't worry, Bobbie. You'll be able to read the article before I submit it, and I'll make any changes you want."

Relief flashed over Bobbie's face. "Thank you."

"Article?" he asked.

"Yes, they've agreed to let me interview them. I know several magazines that would love to have articles about being part of the Bashir royal family."

"And don't worry, I'll clear it through Malik before we do anything," Catherine said, standing.

Khalid nodded. Not that his brother said no to his wife very often.

"Rafi thinks it's a good idea," Bobbie commented.

"I'm sure Hassan will too."

The three women walked out of the room, chatting as they moved. Khalid watched Zoey fiddle with her camera. Why was she nervous? He wanted to talk with her, and they would need some privacy for that. "Would you like to go out into the garden for a bit?"

"That would be great. I've been wanting to explore it."

Khalid took her by the elbow and escorted her into the garden. "You are more than welcome to explore anytime." He'd beefed up security so she would never be alone, even in the garden.

Her grin lit up her face. The moment they were outside, she raised her camera and began taking pictures. He stood and watched her smile play around her lips. This woman was happiest when doing her job.

In a way, she was like him, but Khalid didn't mind staying in one place. With Zoey, he had a feeling it would be like trying to clip the wings of a butterfly. And that was something he wouldn't do.

"So anything exciting happen while I was out with Rafi, Bobbie, and Zain?" she asked as she took pictures of the flowers and garden paths.

"Not really." He walked behind her, enjoying the way her body moved.

"Does that mean I can go back to the hotel now?"

Khalid laughed. "Still on that?"

"Yes. Really, do I need to stay here?"

"You do." He waited until she'd lowered her camera before leading her over to the gazebo. Here they would have some privacy. He guided her up the stairs and then motioned for her to take a seat.

"What has happened?" She put her camera down on the bench and stared at him.

"What makes you think something has happened?" He sat down and turned toward her. Her silver eyes were filled with concern.

"Well, you obviously wanted to talk to me and found someplace private."

"I did." Her straight talk made his lips curve up. She wasn't one to beat around the bush. He reached over and took her hand in his. "This isn't about why it's ill-advised for you to leave. Tell me you don't feel it."

"Feel what?"

"This connection between us." He threaded his fingers through hers. "When we kissed I wanted nothing more than to carry you to my room and spend time learning your wants and desires."

Her cheeks turned pink, and her lips parted. His instincts were right. She did feel something for him.

"And if I do feel this connection?" Her voice was soft.

"Then let's explore it. I can't do that if you're in a hotel." She let out a laugh, and he continued. "We'd have more privacy."

"Would we?"

She wasn't shooting him down. "No one would dare invade my rooms. But at a hotel?" He shook his head.

"If I agree to this?"

"We'll take things one step at a time." His desire flared. "You liked what I did this morning with the rope."

"Yes." Her silver eyes flared with heat, and he tightened his hand around hers.

"Would you like to explore more?" He would only take this as far as she wanted. It wasn't like he needed kink in his life. He knew his brothers enjoyed some form of kink, but for him, shibari was enough.

She swallowed. "Ummm." Her cheeks turned red.

"Tell me, Zoey." He kept his voice low and deep.

"I don't mind a little kink."

"Explain what you mean, please?"

She shook her head. "This is not a talk I thought I'd be having today."

He let out a small laugh. "I didn't either, but you've been in my head all day. Interfering with my work. I want to explore what is between us. I want to explore with you. I want to explore you."

Where were the words coming from? He had never waxed poetic before. He also had never showed his heart as he was right now. There was something about Zoey that called to him, something that made him want more than just a casual relationship with her.

"Oh, Khalid. I want that too." She leaned forward, and her lips brushed his cheek before she whispered in his ear, "Kink-wise, mainly I want to explore more bondage and toys. And I'd love to be your shibari model."

Lust roared through his body, and he barely held himself back from dragging her into his lap and having his way with her right there in the gazebo. "We'll take this slowly."

"I'd like that. I don't have much experience."

He stared at her upturned face and waited. There was more, he was sure of it.

"I'm not a virgin, but I haven't had many relationships. My job doesn't lend itself to it."

"Like mine does." He smiled at her. "It's been a while for me. As I said, we'll take this slowly and together." He cupped her chin and brushed his lips over hers.

A clearing of a throat had him moving back. He turned toward the sound.

"Sorry, Khalid," Ryan said, standing at the bottom of the gazebo steps. "Jahir has found something."

Khalid sighed. "Sorry, sweetheart." He brushed his lips over hers.

"Go. Do your job."

He stood, then gave her another hard kiss before dropping her hand and walking away. For the first time in his life, he didn't want to do his job.

The next two days passed quickly. After Ryan had interrupted them, Khalid hadn't had time to spend with Zoey. Jahir had found a money trail from Kalif to outside the country, and they were following it. Unfortunately, the trail had gone cold.

But Malik had already contacted two different countries that the money funneled through. They were on the lookout, so maybe they'd catch a break.

Rafi had talked to the tribal leaders about the symbol. It was indeed an old symbol for peace, and it was cropping up more and more in Bashir City. No one knew how it was getting onto buildings. Whoever was doing it avoided the surveillance cameras. Was there some sort of rebel faction he didn't know about? He'd talked with Ryan about it, but so far they couldn't come up with anything.

Khalid sat down in his office and went over the official list of events for the 300th anniversary. It would happen in a little over a week. There were several parties that the family was expected to attend. At least they were narrowing them down, and only one royal couple would attend each event. The tough one was the parade, which involved the entire family.

A security nightmare. But he'd find a way to keep everyone safe. Any of these events would be perfect for Kalif to attack. But honestly, so far, except for the marketplace attack, Kalif hadn't harmed any locals.

He and his group mainly targeted the family, trying to get them to leave him and his poppy-growing business alone, but that wasn't going to happen. Since the drug rehabilitation wing had opened up at the hospital and Hassan and Sara had started doing outreach, opium was no longer as popular as it had been.

Sara had been right. Education was the answer. Khalid was working on that too. Talking with the people, advising them what to watch out for and whom to call. The Bashir City police force, which had been very small, maybe ten men, was now a full force of seventy-five. Along with Khalid's security force of fifty, things were moving along quite well. The country was blossoming more than ever. Now to keep Kalif and his men from throwing them all back into the dark ages.

"I figured I'd find you here."

Khalid looked up to see Zoey standing in the doorway. Zoey. In the days they'd been apart he'd reined in his protective instincts and allowed her to go out with Habib around the city. Of course, he'd been in the city working as well, just in case something happened.

"Come on in." He waved her over, took her hand, and stared at it, thinking of the shibari knots he'd tied the other day. "What can I do for you?" He was upset they hadn't been able to spend more time together, but his job and hers kept them both busy.

"Sara and Bobbie mentioned a restaurant in town, and I was wondering if it would be possible for us to visit it?"

What were Sara and Bobbie up to? "And what is the name of this restaurant?"

"Wafi's. They said it was a local hangout, and I'd really like to check it out."

That made sense. Wafi's would appeal to Zoey and be great for her article. "I see no reason why not. Let me call Wafi and let him know we'll be there tonight."

Zoey smiled. "I better go change." She turned and disappeared. Khalid couldn't help but grin. Such a small gesture made her happy. He wondered what else would make her smile like that.

He looked at the folder on his desk marked with her name. Like everyone who came into the royal household, he had had her investigated. But he hadn't read the report. Instead, he'd handed it to Ryan and asked him to look for anything he needed to know.

Ryan told him the report was clean. But that didn't mean Khalid wasn't curious. Maybe over dinner he'd get her to open up about her life. Because he wanted to learn more about the woman he wanted in his life.

$\sim$

After they were seated, side by side, Zoey looked around Wafi's in delight. She'd have to talk with the owner about coming back and taking some pictures. She'd left her camera at the palace on purpose, wanting to take in the atmosphere of the place before she started photographing it. After she'd submitted her first article on Bashir, the magazine wanted more. And her first blog post ... she'd never had so many hits and comments.

People were curious about this tiny country, and Zoey couldn't blame them. She was enjoying her time here, and a certain man as well. She glanced at Khalid from beneath her lashes.

This dark, mysterious man. The cliché fit. Zoey had a feeling there was a lot more to Khalid than what he'd showed. She'd noticed he let his guard down a bit when it was just family, but most of the time, he was always alert.

She was also aware he didn't sleep a lot. Four days ago, she'd discovered she was sharing his wing, and his room was next to hers. The same night, she'd jolted from a nightmare. Unable to fall back asleep, she'd gone out onto the balcony to calm herself. The lights had been on in his room, shining out the balcony doors.

Was he awake because he was worried? Working? Or did nightmares plague him too? Hers were from Iraq. Even though most of the time she'd been in a peaceful town or situation, a couple of times, insurgents had set off bombs. She'd gotten caught close to them twice. The military psychologist had told her their effects would lessen in time, and they would.

The other night, when she'd been up, she'd seen Khalid outside on the balcony. It had been four in the morning. If she worked in the sitting room, she used the small lamp she left on at night, or she worked in her bedroom. She didn't want to advertise she was up. But that night, she'd waited to see if Khalid would knock on her door. He hadn't, so she'd figured he wasn't even aware she was up.

"Prince Khalid, Lady Zoey," the waiter said, jerking her back to the present. "I am very happy to have you here tonight." A small man came up to the table, setting down water and glasses.

"Thank you, Wafi," Khalid said.

"I have a special menu tonight. Will you allow me to choose for you?"

Khalid looked at her. "That's fine with me. It would be a pleasure."

The older man beamed. "Good choice. Do you want wine with dinner?"

"Zoey?" Khalid asked.

"I'm fine without it."

"No wine, but some of your delicious fruit juice would be most welcome."

"Of course. My job is to make your meal the best it can be." He turned and left.

Three hours later, Zoey sat back with a groan. "I can't eat another bite."

Khalid laughed. "Wafi pulled out all the stops tonight."

"It was very good." Zoey glanced at Khalid. "You're more relaxed tonight." There were no lines of strain around his lips.

"Probably because the family is at home, and Ryan and the others are outside Wafi's."

"Always on duty."

"Yes." He leaned back and stretched his arm over the back of the booth. His hand caressed her shoulder. "Tell me about Zoey."

"Me? There isn't much to tell."

"Oh, I think there is. I've noticed you don't like being told what to do."

Zoey laughed. "Who does?"

He nodded and stared at her with those penetrating dark eyes.

Zoey let out a sigh. "My parents were very overprotective of me."

She really didn't want to talk about her parents, but if they were going to have any sort of relationship, he needed to understand why she chafed at his protective stance.

"Most parents are. Even mine were protective of us boys."

"Not like mine." Zoey drew circles on the tabletop with her finger. "I was allowed to go to school, but Mom or Dad walked me to and from. I wasn't allowed to do any afterschool activities. Heck, I don't think I ever had a friend over to our house."

Khalid frowned. "That is no way for a child to grow up. My parents were protective, but we were allowed to be children, and I had brothers."

"I'm glad you had brothers to play with. I had no one, and it only got worse when I was a teenager."

"They were afraid you'd rebel."

"Probably. You know, I never dated until I left for college, and even then it wasn't until I was a junior." She'd been so unsure of herself as a woman. Thank goodness she'd had some good female friends in college who had helped her.

"Why were your parents so overprotective?" He caressed the back of her neck in a soothing motion.

"I don't know. They never told me. I've suspected for years they had a child before I was born and something happened."

Khalid frowned. Why were her parents so secretive? He didn't like this. Maybe he'd better read that report after all. "They never talked about it?" While his father had kept some things quiet, his parents were open, as were the rest of the family. Yes, there were things they didn't talk about, but that was by mutual agreement.

"Not to me." She took a sip of water from her glass. "And to be honest, I've never asked as I didn't want to upset them."

"So tell me about these languages you know how to speak." He didn't like how uncomfortable she was. "Habib is very impressed." Time to change the subject, but knowing how she felt about her parents helped him understand why she chafed so much at his protectiveness.

A smile played around her lips. "Well, I lived in California, and we had a lot of kids who spoke Spanish at school, so I started with

Spanish. It was fun and I picked it up. So I kept learning more languages."

"Something you could do by yourself." He was getting the picture. She had been alone a lot, and this was something she could do to please herself.

"Yes, when I was in high school, I discovered photography. That was something I could do in my own backyard, so to speak."

"How did you become a travel blogger?" He shook his head at the waiter before he could interrupt. He had Zoey talking, and he wanted to keep her talking.

"By accident." She let out a laugh. "After college I went to work for a Fortune 500 company as one of their translators. I was able to travel and use the languages I'd learned. But it bothered me that I never had a lot of time to investigate the local area I was in."

He nodded and traced the back of her neck. She didn't pull away. Instead shivers of what he assumed was anticipation echoed with each caress.

"Sometimes I would only have a half day, so I would go out with my camera and just start walking."

"Was that safe?" He didn't like the idea of her walking around in unfamiliar places alone.

"Most of the time, yes." She let out a laugh. "Khalid, I'm not reckless, I pay attention and I stick to light, populated areas."

"Go on."

"Well, after a few trips, I started writing a blog, mainly for myself, to journal my travels. The next thing I knew I had followers and people emailing me telling me how much they enjoyed the blog."

"And the corporate job?"

"Stifling at times. Then I had two travel magazines offer me space in their magazines. I was on my way to Japan, so I told them I'd check with the legal department of my company, and if they allowed it I'd submit something after the trip." She paused. "Luckily enough, we had an extra day because of flights and time changes. So I took that day and spent it around Tokyo."

Her silver eyes danced with excitement. Khalid found himself shifting even closer to her.

"Before the flight home, legal gave approval, and I wrote the two travel articles and submitted them along with pictures. I figured they'd turn them down, but to my surprise they didn't."

"Were they the same article?"

"No. I choose difference aspects of Tokyo for each article. And they were both a hit. My blog started getting more traffic, and the travel magazines offered me money to advertise their magazines in my blog."

"You were becoming an entrepreneur."

"Kind of." She shook her head. "I didn't plan it that way. The corporate job was getting to me, so I decided to quit."

"How did you survive?" He couldn't see her going back to her parents after all she'd told him.

"The corporate job paid very well, and since I wasn't home a lot, I didn't have a lot of expenses. I'd saved most of my salary. It wasn't a hardship."

"Good." He didn't want to think about her struggling. "So how long have you been freelancing?"

"For almost two years now." She grinned at him. "I love what I do and have fun doing it."

"That is good."

"Khalid, enough about me." Her fingers trailed over his forehead. "How did you become in charge of security for your family?"

"I kind of fell into it, so to speak." Her fingers over his skin sparked his libido. He hadn't thought about how he got put in charge in a long time. "I used to follow the security team around when I was a teenager, wanting to learn what they did and why."

"Didn't you have a bodyguard?"

"Yes, but he was only around when I left the palace grounds. We'd always been safe until Kalif." Her fingers caressed his cheek.

"So why security?"

"Since I was the youngest I had to assert myself from an early age."

Zoey let out a giggle. "Oh, yeah, I can see that."

"At school I excelled at critical thinking, problem solving, and phys- ical activities. The old head of security, Gafar, took me under his wing and began to teach me." He shifted in his seat. "Gafar was the one who got me into the UK's special forces training."

"You've had military training? Now, why doesn't that surprise me?"

"I have." He shook off the memories of his last mission, when everything had gone to hell and back. "When I came home, Gafar was ready to retire. I stepped into his place."

"Others weren't upset at not being promoted?"

"No. It surprised me. I fully expected to compete for the job. But those men were more than happy to follow rather than lead." He'd been happy to take over protection of his family. "All has been good until just the last year and a half."

"Kalif and the poppy growing?"

"That and other things. I've been hiring more and more security staff, and beefing up the local police department."

"And then comes this American who takes pictures and causes all sorts of problems."

Khalid laughed. "Not really. Compared to Catherine and Sara, you're not so bad."

"So Bobbie didn't give you any problems?"

"Not as much as the other two, although the same can't be said for my brothers."

"I'd love to hear more."

He shook his head. "A story for another time."

Wafi walked up to the table. "And how was everything?" he asked.

"Delicious," Zoey said.

"It was perfect, Wafi. Thank you." Khalid glanced at his watch. It was going on ten, and they should get back to the palace. "I hate to say it, but it's time for us to head home." Khalid slid out of the booth and held his hand out to Zoey.

"Wafi," Zoey said. "Would you allow me to come back when the restaurant is closed and take some pictures? I'd love to do a story on your restaurant."

"Of course, Lady Zoey. You would be a welcome guest." Wafi's smile lit up the entire restaurant, and Khalid hid his own. Zoey had a way of making people feel special without trying.

"Would tomorrow morning be okay?" She looked from Wafi to him and back.

"Very much so," Wafi said.

"It can be arranged." As much as he wanted to keep her in the palace safe, this was her job. The way she made her money. If he thought she'd allow him to pay for her expenses he'd do it, but Zoey would have his head on a platter if he even suggested it. Instead, he would just make sure she stayed safe.

"Good. I'll see you in the morning around ten, Wafi."

"Very good, Lady Zoey. Prince Khalid." Wafi guided them to the entrance and thanked them again for coming before going back into his restaurant.

Khalid cupped Zoey's elbow and led her past the hostess station and out the door. Flashes went off, and he flinched. Damn it, he should have anticipated this happening. His security team pulled up.

"Prince Khalid, who is the young woman you're dining with?" a reporter yelled.

"We hear she's staying on the palace grounds with you?" another yelled.

"Is this another royal romance?" yet another yelled.

"Khalid?" Her voice shook as she pressed to his side.

Ryan, Habib, and others on his security team did their best to push back the press. Finally they made it to the SUV. He opened the door and motioned Zoey inside. The cameras kept going off, along with the reporters shouting questions. He ignored them. He climbed in beside her and slammed the door.

"What the heck was that about?" she asked, once they were inside the vehicle.

Habib and Ryan climbed in front, and the SUV slowly pulled away.

"Paparazzi, the bane of my family's existence. They seem to always sniff out when one of us is out enjoying ourselves."

"I didn't realize they were a nuisance here in Bashir."

"They became an issue when Malik used Catherine as a shield against them. Since then, they've done nothing but follow us around. They usually leave me alone. But apparently my time is up. Annoying little sand fleas."

Zoey let out a laugh. "It's something you can't control."

"No. As much as I'd like to, I cannot control the media." He tucked her against his side. "Let's forget them." He lowered his head. "Come to my room tonight?" he whispered in her ear.

She inhaled sharply. "Yes."

Anticipation flowed through his veins. The rest of the drive was made in silence. When the vehicle stopped at the steps of the palace, his brothers were waiting for him.

"Oh, this doesn't look good," Zoey commented.

"No, it doesn't." He helped her out of the vehicle, keeping her hand in his. Together they walked up the stairs. If the damn paparazzi were going to publish pictures of him and Zoey with some made-up story, he'd do whatever his brothers suggested. He wasn't going to fight them on the issue. Zoey would be protected.

"We've got an problem," Malik said.

"What else is new?" Khalid ran his hand over his head.

"I'll go find the others," Zoey said.

Khalid lifted her hand to his lips and kissed the back of it before letting her go. Once she was out of earshot, he looked at his brother. "What happened?"

"Kalif raided one of the villages. Security needs to get out there." Malik said.

"Injuries?" Khalid ran his fingers through his hair.

"Yes," Hassan said. "Sara's at the hospital putting packs together and finding volunteers."

"I'm going with Hassan and Sara as extra backup," Rafi said.

Khalid shook his head. "That's too many of us going."

"I know." Rafi placed his hand on Khalid's arm. "But you'll be needed with the security forces, so I'll stay with Hassan and Sara. Less you have to worry about."

His brother made sense, but Khalid didn't like it. He looked at Malik.

"I agreed he could go. I'll be here, like a good king, but I want updates every hour."

Khalid nodded. "All right." He glanced at Hassan and Rafi. "But if I say get the hell out, you will." They both nodded. "Let me get a team together." He turned and jogged down the stairs and toward the bungalows where the security staff would be getting ready. It was going to be a long night.

~

Zoey found Catherine and Bobbie in the family room, neither looking happy. "Hey, what's going on?"

Catherine turned. "Hey, Zoey. Is Khalid with his brothers?"

"Yes. What is going on?" Something was up. Bobbie was normally the bubbly one of the group, and there was worry in her eyes.

"There was an incident in one of the villages," Bobbie said quietly.

"What kind of incident?" Zoey's heart stuttered.

"Kalif attacked. We got word via a short-wave radio call."

"Injuries?" No wonder the brothers looked grim.

"Yes," Malik said, walking into the room. Catherine ran to his side and hugged him. "Bobbie, Rafi's gone up to your rooms."

Bobbie nodded, then left the room. "I don't like this, Malik," Catherine said.

"Like what?" Zoey felt like she was missing a big piece of the conversation.

"Zoey, so sorry," Malik said. "Hassan, Sara, Rafi, Khalid, and a security force are heading out to the village."

"Too many. Rafi should stay here," Catherine said.

"Honey," Malik said, then tilted her head up. "Since Rafi renounced his claim to the throne, I won't stop him from wanting to help, and Khalid will be busy. Rafi will be extra security for Hassan and Sara."

Catherine sighed. "I know."

Several things hit Zoey at once. While she knew about Rafi abdicating his right to the throne, hearing it from Malik made it more real. Hassan and Sara going to the village made sense, and Khalid going with them ... Fear gripped her stomach and twisted. Khalid was going out there to protect his family and the villagers.

Her knees weakened. Zoey sat down hard. Malik's eyes widened.

"I'm sorry, I shouldn't have blurted that out like that," Malik said.

Zoey waved her hand and forced air into her lungs. "Where is Khalid right now?"

"At the bungalows gathering up men to take with them."

Zoey didn't even hesitate; she jumped up and ran. She had to talk to him and now. She barely heard Catherine shouting her name as she ran out the front door and down the stairs.

Khalid was going into danger, and she didn't know if her heart could take it. Especially if there was any chance he wouldn't come back.

Khalid and Ryan looked over the map, deciding on the best road to use and how to protect everyone. Khalid hated the idea of traveling at night, but Hassan insisted. Khalid understood; there were people injured and Hassan wanted to get out there as soon as possible.

"I suggest we send an advance team, let's say six men fully armed and ready for anything. I wouldn't put it past Kalif to lay a trap," Ryan said.

"Yes, it's a three-hour drive. If they leave in the next thirty minutes, that will put them close to an hour ahead of us. Hassan and Sara are getting supplies from the hospital. He's going to contact me when they're ready. I should have insisted we get some helicopters."

"All right, let me go get the advance team together and we'll go. As for the helicopters, we've never needed them, so why waste resources?"

Khalid nodded. Ryan was a good man, but Khalid hated sending his men into an unknown situation with him.

"Zoey," Ryan said as he was leaving.

Khalid looked up as she crossed the room to him. "I ... " She threw herself into his arms.

"Zoey?" She held him tightly as if she never wanted to let him go.

"Malik told me what happened. I don't want you to go, but I know you have to. Be safe, Khalid. Don't take unnecessary chances."

He held Zoey against him with pleasure running through his body. She cared about him. "I won't. I'll be careful." His gut tightened at the thought of never coming back to his Zoey. Yes. The thought surprised him, but he recognized the truth in it. She was his.

"I know you will be." She ran her fingers over his cheek. "But things can get out of control. I want you safe."

"Sweetheart." He lowered his forehead to rest against hers. "I will do my best to come back to you unscathed. I have to go."

"I know, but all I can think about is keeping you out of harm's way."

"Now who is being the overprotective one?" There was laughter in his voice.

"I know." Her arms slid over his shoulders.

Just then his phone rang. Keeping one arm around her, he pulled his cell out. It was Hassan. "Yeah, Hassan. Be there in fifteen minutes." He hung up and stared down at Zoey.

"You have to go." She loosened her hold on him.

"Yes." He tightened his arms around her. "We'll be checking in every hour. We have six satellite phones. Malik will keep you informed."

"Just be careful." She brushed a kiss over his lips.

Khalid wasn't going to let her escape that easily. He lowered his head and captured her lips with his. His tongue traced her lips until she gave him access. Their tongues mingled, tasted, and explored. He would come back to this woman because he wasn't done with her yet.

When they broke apart, both were breathing heavily. "I have to go." He rested his forehead against hers once again. "Stay with Catherine and Bobbie. Habib will be on guard, as will Samir and Hamaz. Do not leave the palace until I return."

"Then you better take care of things quickly." She brushed her fingers over his short hair before stepping back. Then she turned and left the building.

It was one of the hardest things Khalid had ever done, letting her walk away. He caught a glimpse of Habib and some of the tension left his body. Habib would watch over her and the other women. All the bodyguards would.

Khalid gathered up his supplies and weapons and made his way out to the SUVs. These were custom-built SUVs, larger than most so they could carry equipment, but also fitted with special tires for the sand and the harsh back roads. They were also bulletproof. Khalid frowned. Except for the tires.

Throwing his stuff in the back, he looked at Syed, Jahir, Ramir, and Abdulla, who would be driving the vehicles. Then he glanced at the other eight men. With the five men Ryan had gone ahead with, they should have enough.

"We first go to the hospital and load up supplies and personnel, then we'll head out to the village." Khalid paced as he spoke. "All we know is Kalif attacked the village. We don't know with how many men or anything else. Just that there are injuries. So everyone needs to pay attention. Ryan went ahead to scope things out. I will check in with each driver every hour, with Ryan, too, and then report back to our king."

"Yes, sir," the men answered.

"Let's go." Khalid glanced up at the palace before he climbed into his SUV. "Be safe and rest well, my Zoey," he whispered before he seated himself and shut the door.

When the caravan of SUVs faded from her sight, Zoey stepped back from the window.

"Somehow I don't think this was how Khalid planned on spending the night," Bobbie said from her place across the room.

"No, it wasn't." Zoey flashed Bobbie a grin. The best laid plans and all that crap. "How long will it take them to get to the village?" She had to contain her worry. She didn't want to upset the other women.

"About three hours," Catherine answered

Zoey glanced at the clock. It was almost eleven now and would probably take about thirty minutes to load the supplies from the hospital, so it would be at least two in the morning before they got to the village.

"It's going to be a long night."

"Yes," Catherine said. "Come sit down, let's talk more about your work."

~

Zoey jolted awake when someone touched her. "It's just me," Malik said softly.

"Sorry." She must have fallen asleep on the sofa. She glanced over to the other sofas. Catherine was out and so was Bobbie. "What's happening?"

Malik motioned for her to follow him. Zoey stood and tiptoed out of the room. "I don't want to wake Bobbie or Catherine just yet."

"What time is it?" Zoey yawned and stretched.

"Four-thirty. Khalid just checked in again."

The last report had been at two. The convoy had been getting ready to enter the village. So far everything was good. No ambush. Nothing out of place. "And?"

"They've secured the village, and those who have been injured are being treated."

Zoey watched Malik's face as he spoke. His features were tight, and there were lines of tiredness and strain around his eyes and on his forehead. "What else?"

"How do you know there is more?"

"I'm good at reading people. You're too tense." He was, and the fact he was talking to her and not all of them clued her in as well.

Malik shook his head. "I'm only telling you this because Khalid insisted I do so. They've found evidence of bombs in the village."

"Kalif left them?" Damn it. What was wrong with this man? Why was he so insistent on hurting people? It was one thing she would never understand.

"Sorry, I should say bomb making. Khalid is working on getting the full story, but I have a feeling the villagers have been terrorized for a while." He drew his hand over his face.

Zoey placed her hand on his arm. "Malik, you can't control everything." This man took so much on his shoulders.

"No, but I feel like I should." He ran his hand through his hair. "How much has Khalid told you about Kalif?"

"Enough."

Malik nodded. "We agreed that he'll check in again after the sun comes up and they can do a better assessment."

Zoey nodded. Hopefully they wouldn't find anything and could come home right away.

"In the meantime, why don't you get some rest."

"And you?" Zoey yawned.

"I'll wake Bobbie, then carry my wife to bed. I'll catch a catnap and be fine."

"Malik." She touched his arm again. "You are doing a fantastic job. Don't let this one thing get to you."

He nodded, and went back into the family room. Zoey made her way upstairs and into her bedroom. She dropped her clothes on the floor and climbed into bed, but not before she set her alarm for seven-thirty. She wanted to be awake and ready when Khalid called the next time. She curled up and sent a prayer to the heavens. "Keep him safe." I think I'm falling for him.

❈ 8 ❈

Khalid stretched his arms over his head before he glanced around the village. Thank goodness most of the injuries were minor, with only a few serious ones. What concerned him more was the evidence of the bomb making.

One of the village elders told him Kalif had used three of the buildings and forced their young people to help him. But when one of Kalif's men started going after the women, the men had risen up against them.

They'd been outnumbered, but Kalif and his men had run. Khalid rubbed his chin. Why did he run? Probably didn't want a confrontation. From what he'd been able to gather, Kalif only had about thirty men.

Now that it was light, they could see that there was only minor damage to the village, more just injuries from the fight. In a way it was good news.

"Khalid," Rafi said, walking up to his brother.

"Yes, Rafi."

"I talked with several of the young men. It looks like your suspicions were correct. Kalif has moved his operation close to the border."

"Damn." That could become an even more dangerous situation.

He'd have to warn Malik to explain things to their neighboring country. "If he escapes over the border we'll never find him."

"Yeah, but I don't think he's going to run. I think he pulled back to regroup. There's something bigger at play here."

"That's what I keep thinking, but what? And why use the villagers?"

"Because he's running out of men," Ryan said, striding up to the pair. "He's only got about thirty men left, and while we're only a force of let's say twenty here, we have more fire power and a lot more skill."

"Which doesn't make sense," Rafi said. "He had to know we'd come out here."

"True, but ... " Ice filled Khalid's veins. Why hadn't he thought about this? "He's going to try something in Bashir City." He grabbed the sat phone and called Malik. "Malik, Kalif is going to try something in the city. Get—"

Garbled noise froze Khalid in place. Something crashed. People were yelling. "Malik!" Zoey!

"What happened?" Rafi asked.

"The phone went dead."

"Not possible," Ryan said. "It's a sat phone. Is it possible the battery died?"

Khalid dialed the palace but there was no connection. It could just be the battery, but his gut was telling him it was something else. He dialed their headquarters in the city, nothing. Khalid looked at Ryan, who was on his phone. Ryan shook his head. Khalid wasn't going to wait around to figure this out.

"Rafi, get the SUV. We need to get back. Let me talk with Hassan, and then we'll go." Khalid tried to keep calm, but Ryan was right. Sat phones didn't go dead. His gut clenched.

Rafi drove like a formula 500 driver, bouncing them around in the SUV. Khalid wasn't happy leaving Hassan and Sara in the village, but he'd left most of the security force there, along with Sara's bodyguard, Najah.

Khalid finally got through to security at the palace. A bomb had been set off in the city. Communications were out everywhere. He explained that they'd already left the village, but it would take them time to get back. He should have insisted on getting a couple of helicopters.

"Hold on," Rafi said, a second before the vehicle went airborne, then bounced back to the ground.

"Damn it, Rafi, getting us killed won't help." He rubbed his head where it had hit the roof.

"That was unexpected," Rafi said. "I'll get us there in one piece."

Ryan sat in the front seat with Rafi, his features grim as he held on for dear life. Why hadn't he'd seen this for what it was, a way to lure them away from the city? Kalif wasn't stupid, but then again, why attack the city?

The anniversary celebration. Kalif wanted to make a statement. Well, Khalid would be damned if he'd let Kalif get away with this. At least Zoey and his family were safe in the palace. Security was in place and tight.

Zoey was just coming down the stairs when the palace shuddered. What the hell? That wasn't an earthquake.

Habib ran to the bottom of the stairs along with the other bodyguards. "Lady Zoey."

"I'm fine. What was that?"

"A very large explosion," Samir, Catherine's bodyguard, said.

Zoey reached the bottom of the stairs as Malik came running down the hall. "Stay with the women, Habib. No one is to leave the palace."

"Where are you going?" Zoey asked.

"We have some security staff still here. I need to get them into Bashir City. The hospital is on alert."

"Malik," Zoey called to him. "I'm coming with you."

"Zoey."

She held up her hand. "You need every person you can get right now. I'm trained in first aid."

He shook his head, but she followed him out of the palace with Habib on their six to meet with the security men near the bungalows.

Zoey stood her ground with Malik. "I'm going to go help." She helped load supplies into the back of the SUV.

"Zoey, Khalid would kill me if something happened to you." He rubbed the back of his neck.

"I'll be fine. Habib will be with me. You need someone in town besides security who can report back to you. You can't go, you are the king and a lot more valuable."

"Khalid might have something to say about that," Malik muttered.

"He might. But the people in town have seen me around, they sort of know me. I can be the eyes and ears for you. Plus, with my first-aid training, I can help the people."

"She's right, sir," Habib said. "Zoey has been among the people. They trust her. While I have to agree Khalid won't like it, seeing her will boost the people's confidence."

"Damn it, all right. But don't take any unnecessary chances. A security force will take you in. The other team is helping the doctors and nurses from the hospital."

Zoey wanted to high-five Habib, but she nodded. "I need to change." She needed her boots, at a minimum.

Malik opened the door to the SUV. "Get in, they'll drive us up to the palace, and you can change."

Zoey jumped in and within a minute they were at the entrance to the palace. Malik walked with her up the stairs. "I really don't like this, Zoey," he said.

"I'll be careful. Kalif is trying to scare everyone. A friendly face will help." Zoey walked into the entryway to see Catherine and Bobbie. "How much did you hear?"

"Enough." Catherine crossed over to her and hugged her. "Be safe."

Zoey took a deep breath and hugged her back. "I will be."

"I want to go with you," Bobbie said.

"You have Zain to take care of," Zoey said. The little boy was just now starting to come out of his shell. She didn't mind risking her own life, but she wouldn't risk the other women in the family.

"And Rafi would kill me if something happened to you," Malik added.

"You think Khalid won't?" Catherine asked, moving to her husband's side.

"He won't, because nothing is going to happen to me. Now, if you'll excuse me." Zoey didn't wait for an answer. She sprinted up the stairs. Once in her room, she pulled on a pair of jeans, a long-sleeved shirt, and her boots.

Within five minutes she was on her way into Bashir City. When they reached the outskirts, she could see the chaos. People were out on the street everywhere. Many looked shell- shocked.

The vehicles stopped, and everyone jumped out. Medical personnel were already on the scene. Zoey stayed out of their way, but she stopped and talked to people. Calming them down, checking out if they were injured, and calling over medical staff, if needed. She talked with them, finding out what they'd seen or heard. She assured them everything was fine, King Malik had everything under control.

It amazed her what her words did for the people. They smiled, gave her hugs, and told her to be safe. Even though Habib stayed by her side, the people never shied away. They were happy to see her and were more than willing to talk to her.

So far, there had only been a few serious injuries, and she hoped it stayed that way. Most people were just frightened by the noise. She nodded to Habib, and they made their way toward the area where the bomb had gone off.

"We need to be careful, Lady Zoey," Habib said.

"I'm keeping my eyes and ears open." She wouldn't put it past this Kalif guy to have left men or more explosives behind.

From what people had told her, the bomb had been set off at the edge of the marketplace, and with it being so early, no one was there yet. Lucky break? Maybe. Zoey wondered, though; this was the second bomb that had gone off where there weren't a lot of people. If it had gone off two hours later, the marketplace would have been filled.

Zoey looked at each building as they walked. More and more the symbol popped up. Peace. Someone else didn't like what Kalif was doing. The eerie quietness made the hair on the back of her neck rise.

"Lady Zoey, please stop," Habib said, grasping her by the arm.

"Habib, what is it?" Zoey glanced around, trying to see what he was seeing.

"Something doesn't feel right." He motioned to the three men with them. "We need to go back."

Zoey nodded. The security force surrounded her and Habib, and they slowly made their way back in the other direction. Just as they made it to the corner, a shot rang out.

The men swore, and Habib grasped Zoey by the arm. "Run," he said.

Zoey didn't hesitate. Together they ran until they were back on the main street and there were lots of people. And no more shots rang out.

Zoey turned to see only Habib with her. "Where is the security?" she asked, trying to catch her breath. Wow, she really needed to do some more cardio. Her heart was pounding more from the run than being frightened. While the shots hadn't even been close, an icy shiver slid over her spine.

"They are taking care of the situation. Come, Lady Zoey, we must get you to safety." Habib urged her to move.

Zoey wanted to dig in her heels but didn't. Habib was only following orders, as was the rest of the security force. Thankfully, no one was shooting at them now, or at the people on the streets who were now angry that Kalif had bombed their city again.

The fact that this wasn't the first bombing got to Zoey. She wanted to find this Kalif guy and pound him into the ground. A flash caught her eye, and she turned to see a set of photographers. Oh, hell, no.

Zoey pulled her arm from Habib and marched up to the press. "Put those cameras away."

They stared at her, so she repeated her words in Arabic. Jaws dropped open, but they lowered their cameras.

"Lady Zoey, will you give us an interview?" a man called out.

"Are you crazy?" Zoey shook her head. "Listen, guys, I know you're doing your job, but a bomb just went off. These people need help, not cameras, and not interviews. If you can't be helpful, then leave so others can." She hated how mercenary some reporters were. Paparazzi, Khalid called them.

"But Lady Zoey, we need to report."

"You need to be respectful." It was one thing Zoey hated about some reporters and why she was always so careful. When people were hurting you needed to respect their privacy and their needs. "You don't thrust a camera or a microphone in someone's face when they are hurting or injured."

Many reporters had that kind of respect, but others didn't. Even when Zoey was in war-torn areas, she set up her interviews at the convenience of the person she was taking to, never at their expense, and only if they were ready.

One of the reporters stepped forward. "I'm a trained medic, what do you need?"

Zoey let out a sigh. "People are frightened, please just go reassure them. And be careful."

Several of the reporters nodded, and moved toward the people, talking to them in low voices. Others just shook their heads and moved away.

"Lady Zoey," Habib said.

"Yes, Habib." She was glad to see the paparazzi moving away. At least they were being respectful. Maybe they weren't as bad as she had been led to believe.

"Prepare yourself."

Before she could ask why, she turned to see Khalid barreling up the street with Rafi and Ryan right next to him. No wonder the paparazzi had fled. Khalid's face looked as if it was carved out of stone. Angry stone.

"Zoey," he bellowed. "What are you doing here? You weren't supposed to leave the palace."

Zoey shook her head. What a way to bring attention to them. "Calm down, would you," she said when he reached her side.

"Calm down?" He grasped her by the arms as if he wanted to shake her. "Can you imagine my worry when I finally got through to Malik and he tells me you're in town?" He turned to Habib. "Get her back to the palace."

"No." Zoey dug her heels in, metaphorically. "Khalid," she softened her tone. "I'm fine. The people need reassurance."

"We'll take care of it," Rafi said.

Just then Ryan's radio went off. They all listened. The security force had found the shooter, but he was already dead.

"Shooter?" Khalid's fingers tightened. "You were shot at?"

"Not really." She looked down at the ground.

Khalid let out a growl that was the only thing she could think of when it reached her ears. "Not really? That's it."

The next thing she knew, Khalid was lifting her into his arms. "Habib, let's go. Rafi, Ryan, be right back." He walked briskly down the road.

"Khalid, put me down." His arms were like tempered iron around her. Talk about caveman tactics.

"No."

Zoey wiggled, and Khalid tightened his hold on her. He lowered his head until his lips were by her ear. "Behave, or I'll punish you."

In addition to her being outraged at his hefting her into his arms in front of everyone, a flash of desire went through her body at his whispered words. Oh, this was so not the time. She wanted to be angry with him, but she understood his need for protection, and for protecting her. Khalid stopped and he lowered her to her feet. He pulled open the door of the SUV, then lifted her inside.

"I ... " He slammed the door before she could say more, and Habib got in front with the driver. Khalid spoke sharply to the driver, shut the door, and they were off.

She glared at Khalid, but he couldn't see her through the tinted windows. Oh, when he got back to the palace, they were going to talk.

Zoey paced around her bedroom waiting for Khalid to return. She was so angry. She could take care of herself, but the man didn't have a clue.

"Zoey," Bobbie said, poking her head inside the doorway.

"What?" Bobbie took a step back, and Zoey's remorse was immediate. "I'm sorry. I'm angry, but I shouldn't take it out on you."

"I understand. Our men can be very frustrating. Malik is going to give us an update, do you want to come downstairs for it?"

"Yes." Zoey wanted to know what was going on. The women went to Malik's office, where he and Catherine waited.

"Here's what I know. There were injuries, some serious and some not, at the village. Hassan, Sara, and part of the security forces are on their way back. The village is secure, as some of the security force has stayed."

"Well, that's good news," Bobbie said.

"Yes. The bomb in the marketplace only caused minor injuries, plus all the damage. The area is secure and cleanup is beginning. As for the shooter," he said, then glanced at Zoey, "when the security force found him, he was dead. Apparently someone shot the shooter, and it wasn't us."

"Distract and divide," Zoey muttered. She'd reported the information about the injuries to Malik when she'd arrived back.

Malik's eyes narrowed.

"Sorry, just something I remembered from one of the military guys I worked with in Iraq." Zoey ran her hand over her face. "Distract and divide the enemy. But in this case I think Kalif did that to us."

"Yes," Malik said. "We fell into that trap. We sent everyone to the village and left the city vulnerable."

"Or he hoped you would be vulnerable," Zoey said.

"But what is his end game?" Catherine asked, moving closer to her husband.

"I wish I knew," Malik said.

Zoey leaned back in her chair. "There has to be something he wants and wants bad enough to kill over." She'd seen this time and time again in some of the war-torn areas of the world. "Power?"

Malik shook his head. "He has no power without people to follow him. The people have already denounced him."

"Maybe the poppy fields," Catherine said.

"We've destroyed almost all of them," Malik commented.

Zoey rubbed her nose. "I know poppies can be used to make opium."

"And smoked as well," Hassan said, entering the room with Sara. Hugs and kisses were given before they took seats.

"So you've destroyed most of the poppy fields. You said the people won't follow Kalif, but are there others? He has to have some sort of following." Zoey was logically trying to think this through. There had to be something this guy wanted.

"Maybe in the beginning, when he was still involved with the tribal leaders, but they disavowed him a while ago. They would never act out against the people of Bashir."

"But he's got men. The ones who followed me, someone who ransacked my room, and someone shot out the tire. I'm assuming it's Kalif behind those."

"No assumptions." Malik shook his head. "The men following you were Kalif's, so was the man who broke into your room, and probably the shooter."

"All right." Zoey stood up and paced, working this all through her mind. "Has the royal family been targeted before this?" They all looked at each other and then back at her. "I'm going to take that as a yes."

Malik sat back in his chair. "Kalif has done some things in the past. Sometimes there's evidence that points in his direction, other times not so much."

"But we've always suspected," Hassan said.

"Khalid has thought about it," Zoey said, remembering how he was the one who had said it was Kalif from the beginning.

"This is going to take some thought and time to figure out. But Zoey seems to be right. Kalif is trying to divide the people, and I won't have it," Malik said.

"I know the country's anniversary event is due to start soon," Zoey said.

"Yes, as Khalid says, it's a security nightmare," Malik said.

"Maybe not." Zoey rubbed her nose. "What if you tell the people what is going on?"

Malik stared at her. "Explain what you mean?"

"Go on national television or whatever you do to get the word out to the people of Bashir. Tell them about Kalif's efforts and enlist the people's help."

Malik rubbed his face. "That has merits, but wouldn't it give Kalif more of a platform?"

"Maybe, and then again, maybe not," Hassan said. "The people are aware that Kalif is a troublemaker; we haven't been quiet about what he's doing in the villages and our getting rid of the poppy fields."

"People were angry in town about the bombings," Zoey added.

"I don't want the people of Bashir more afraid than they already are," Malik said.

"That's why sometimes it takes telling them the truth." Zoey ran her hands down her legs. "Let me ask you this, how did you find out about the problems in the villages?"

"By accident," Hassan answered. "Sara and I were visiting one when we found out."

"And how did the people react?" Zoey started looking at this from all sides.

"They were relieved," Sara said.

"But not all." Hassan ran his hands over his face. "Some of the old people don't see an issue in the old ways."

"Which is why I haven't said anything. Do we risk alienating our older population?"

"You're rebuilding your country and keeping them safe," Zoey said. "Sometimes you have to be direct and lay it all on the line."

"It's a great idea," Bobbie said.

"It is. The people of Bashir love the family," Catherine chimed in.

"They do," Malik agreed. "All right. I think this is a good idea, but this announcement should come from Khalid; as head of security, he can explain it better."

Zoey blew out a breath. She hoped Khalid didn't mind her putting him in the spotlight. "And Khalid might kill me for this one, but the family needs to be seen out among the people."

Hassan laughed. "Yeah, he's going to hate that idea, but I think you're right, Zoey."

"We have been out among the people," Malik commented.

"Not in a while," Catherine countered. "Not since our wedding."

"The rest of us have been too busy," Bobbie said.

"If we're seen out and about, the people will have more confidence the family has everything under control," Sara said.

"Agreed." Malik shuffled a couple of files on his desk and pulled out a list. "These are all the anniversary events. As soon as Rafi and

Khalid get back, we'll go over them and divvy them up among all of us."

Zoey blew out a breath. Khalid wasn't going to be happy.

"Are you crazy?" Khalid asked three hours later, as everyone sat around the dining room table. Food and drink had been brought in. Malik had told Khalid they were going to split up the anniversary party events among the four bothers and make appearances with their wives, fiancées, or girlfriends.

"No, I'm not crazy," Malik said, waving his hand at the food. "Everyone grab something. I know we're all probably hungry."

"I'm not going to send the family out in four different directions," Khalid said as he got some food.

Zoey poured herself some coffee and took a plate of fruit. She wasn't really hungry. Anxiety did that to a person, or at least to her. Khalid had arrived back at the palace with Rafi and Ryan thirty minutes ago. Her anger at his sending her back was long gone, especially since she had been able to help the family figure things out.

"I'm not asking you to, but you will do as *your king* says."

All fourteen people in the room went silent. The brothers, their fiancées and Malik's wife, Khalid and Zoey. Ryan and the bodyguards, Habib, Najah, Samir, Hamaz, and Jahir, who stood near the door.

The room stayed silent until everyone grabbed something, Malik looked over at Khalid, who sat down beside Zoey. "Kalif is trying to scare everyone into believing we're hiding behind the palace gates."

Zoey almost choked on the fruit she was eating. She hadn't said that, but maybe Malik had found out something she didn't know?

"They know we care. I was just in the city." Khalid ran his hand over his hair.

"We've become reactionary. We only respond when something happens; we really haven't been out and about," Catherine said.

"Zoey and I were just at Wafi's," Khalid said.

"For dinner, not to meet the people. Zoey's actually been around our people more than we've been in the past few weeks," Rafi said.

"With good reason." Khalid's gaze went around the table. "Kalif is trying to kill us."

"But you've kept us safe, Khalid," Sara mentioned.

"I have. So far." He looked at Malik. "Malik, this is crazy. I agreed to the parade, and two of the events, but for us to go to other events, it will be a security nightmare."

"Ryan," Malik looked at him.

"Yes, sir."

"Do you agree with Khalid's assessment?"

Ryan swallowed.

"Honey, you're putting him on the spot in front of the man he works for," Catherine said.

"Technically he works for me since I pay all the bills."

Khalid nodded. "It's okay, Ryan. Speak freely. I value your opinion."

"Well, sir, I do agree that security will have to be tightened around the family when they go out. The parade has its own nightmarish issues."

"Is it doable?" Malik asked.

Ryan looked at Khalid, then said, "It can be done with the help of the bodyguards and some cooperation from everyone."

Khalid stiffened beside her, and Zoey grasped his hand and gave his fingers a squeeze. "What are you thinking, Ryan?" she asked.

"Each woman here has her own bodyguard. That will help keep each of them safe. If we preview each venue ahead of time, place security at strategic locations, and plan for one couple at each, I don't see a reason why we can't keep everyone safe. We have the manpower."

Zoey glanced at Khalid. His eyes narrowed, then he let out a sigh. "Ryan is right. We do have the men, and if we do a lot of preplanning, we can make it work." She squeezed again, and he turned his hand so their fingers entwined.

Malik's mouth dropped open. "That's it? You're agreeing with us?"

Khalid chuckled and Zoey relaxed. He might have been upset at the beginning, but now he wasn't. "I'd love to order everyone to stay in, but I understand we have a duty as the royal family. The people of Bashir must come first."

"True," Malik said quietly. "Now that's settled, let's narrow down the list of events. There is no way we can make them all, but let's decide the top ten and go from there."

Khalid found Zoey several hours later in the garden. "Zoey," he said sitting down next to her and putting his arm around her shoulders.

"How are you doing?" she asked, snuggling up to his side. "I know this isn't easy for you."

"Ryan was right. It's my own fears that make me keep the family safe." His stomach tightened. He wasn't sure this was the right thing, but then, it was their duty as the royal family.

"But you're still worried. Why?"

"Things happen. Some things that can't be controlled." His military training in England had taught him that.

"That is true." She laid her head on his shoulder. "But I know you and Ryan are trained for this. Have faith in your ability, Khalid."

"I do." It was the unknown he didn't have faith in. Khalid palmed his forehead, trying to still the headache working to take hold. He needed to let this go. To focus on something else, like the lazy pattern Zoey's fingers were doodling on his thigh. For now, he was going to enjoy having Zoey cuddled up to his side and touching him. "I'd like to talk about us."

"Us." Her voice rose, and when she would have moved away from him, he tightened his arm around her.

"Yes. Will you come to my room tonight and enjoy some rope bondage with me?"

Her cheeks turned pink. "I thought you'd never ask."

His lips turned up. "Things have been a little crazy."

"That's the truth."

"Tell me how you learned about shibari?"

"I watched a couple of demonstrations when I was in Japan."

"You enjoyed it."

"Yes. It's very beautiful and erotic."

"That it is. Kinky relationships?"

"Not really. Mainly just holding my hands over my head and spanking."

Khalid nodded. He wasn't into heavy-duty kink. He did enjoy tying women up and spankings, though. She had mentioned toys the other day when they'd talked. He'd have to get some. Shibari was his passion, something to quiet his mind and help him think. But he also enjoyed the emotional high he got when a sub let go and put herself into his hands.

"We'll start with a small bit of shibari tonight, then work our way up to other things. Do you have a safe word?"

"Bunny."

He blinked. "Bunny." He fought to keep the laughter out of his voice.

"It's not like I'd normally yell bunny in the middle of sex."

"That is true." He brushed his lips over her forehead. They sat there for a while, just taking in the soothing sounds of the gardens and holding each other. Then he rose to his feet; taking Zoey's hand, he led her up to his room.

Anticipation flowed through his veins as she stood in his suite. "Do you want to do this in my room or yours?" he asked.

"What is better for you?" Her silver eyes were bright with what he guessed was excitement.

"Let's go my room." She'd be more comfortable in there. He wasn't going to go full- blown shibari on her, not yet. Khalid took her hand in his and led her to his bedroom, pulling her into his arms.

Zoey turned her face up to his and their lips met. The soft, passionate kiss made his cock jump. She was pure temptation in his arms. He broke the kiss and trailed his lips to her ear.

"Undress while I get my materials."

"Yes ... Sir."

The 'sir' caused his dick to pulse with need. It had been a long time since anyone had called him that in this kind of situation. Khalid went to his closet and pulled out his bag that contained his rope and materials.

He turned and his mouth watered. Zoey had removed her blouse and bra. Large breasts with rosy nipples made his fingers itch. "You don't need to take anything else off." His voice was gruff. This woman heated his blood to the boiling point.

"Is something wrong? Umm, Sir." Zoey stood with her clothes in her hands.

"No. You are perfect." Khalid crossed to her, took her clothing and tossed it on the chair. He cupped her breasts. "If you forget to address me as Sir, it's fine. We haven't played together before, and I'm not that hard-core."

Zoey let out a moan at his touch, and he hid a smile. Full, round, and all his. He toyed with her nipples until they were taut, and she shifted from one foot to the other.

"I want to bind your breasts. Is that okay?" He dropped a kiss on the curve of each luscious globe.

"All right." Her voice was shaky, but her body was flushed and her eyes bright.

"Stay right there." Khalid dropped to a knee, opened his bag, and began pulling out his rope and safety equipment. He rose with several different lengths of hemp rope in his hand.

He ran his fingers over the rope. His nerves instantly calmed, and he was centered. "Since this is our first time together. I won't make it very complicated."

Zoey nodded, her gaze on his hands as he uncoiled the rope and stepped towards her.

"Have you ever had an injury to your back? Arms? Chest?"

"No."

"If you start to go numb anywhere let me know."

"I will."

Her voice was soft, but there was a slight tremble to it. Khalid cupped her chin with his free hand and lifted her face until he could see into her eyes. They were still bright but clear.

"It's important, Zoey. I'm not going to tie anything too tight, but sometimes I can hit a pressure point or a nerve even when I try not to."

"I understand." She shifted from one foot to the other again.

"Good." Khalid stepped in front of her and held up the rope. "This is hemp, it's the best rope, and I like to use it for this. It might feel a little rough against your skin, but it won't cause abrasions."

Zoey nodded and took a deep breath as Khalid's arms encircled her and the rope touched her back. Her nerves tingled when the rope made contact with her skin. Earlier, when he'd kissed her, her body had come alive. Now it was like every single nerve anticipated his touch.

His hands adjusted the rope before coming around to her front. He wound the rope over the top of her breasts, and then behind her, and over again. He was right. The rope wasn't uncomfortable.

The way his fingers danced over her skin as he moved the rope into the position he wanted shot flames of desire through her. His concentration was on her and somehow that helped her relax and let go.

She'd never really given up full control in the bedroom before, but with Khalid it seemed to come naturally. Her breathing deepened as he continued his rope play. Round and round. Zoey kept her gaze straight ahead.

The pressure on her breasts increased. Not painfully, but her breasts felt fuller; compressed might be a better word. She fought not to look. Her nipples were standing at attention, and her clit pulsed.

This was way more sensual than she'd imagined. The sure touch of Khalid's hands, the rope against her skin, and his calm breathing put her into a state of relaxation.

"Are you doing all right?" he asked.

"Yes, Sir. Fine."

"Put your hands behind your back."

A shiver went through her body at his words. She obeyed. His fingers encircled her left wrist.

"Relax and let me move your arm."

She took a deep breath and made her arm go lax.

"Very good." His warm breath brushed her shoulder as he bent her arm at the elbow. Rope encircled her wrist, before she could think about it, his fingers were at her right hand. This time she stayed relaxed.

Khalid stepped in front of her, and Zoey tugged at her hands. They were bound behind her. A sense of vulnerability flowed through her veins, then she looked at Khalid.

His dark eyes were filled with passion and need. Trust in him allowed her muscles to go lax, and she could only stare at him. "So beautiful." He stripped off his shirt.

Zoey's mouth went dry. Damn, this man was ripped. The muscles on his chest danced as he threw his shirt to the chair. His deep bronze skin made her think of soft desert sand at sunset. Her gaze continued down to where his pants rested low on his hips.

He had a smattering of dark hair peeking out and there was a distinct bulge behind the fabric. Her gaze traveled back up his body until she met his eyes. Fire and desire burned in those dark eyes of his.

"Still with me?"

Zoey blinked. Then realized what he was asking. "Yes, I'm fine, Sir."

"Good." Khalid stepped closer until his chest brushed against her nipples. She had barely processed the sensations when his warm fingers cupped her face as he lowered his lips to her.

She opened her mouth to his questing tongue. As they kissed he rubbed his chest against hers. Her nipples tightened further, and her pussy twitched. This man was just kissing and rubbing his body against hers, and yet, her body was on fire.

His lips left hers and trailed down her neck, past the rope to her nipples. He enveloped the first one in his hot mouth.

Zoey cried out, her head falling back at the sensation of his tongue flicking her nipple. She tugged at her hands, but they were bound well. When he moved to the other one, her knees wobbled. The sensations coursing through her body made her light-headed. Or maybe it was the man himself.

His arm slid around her waist, holding her up as he nipped and sucked her nipple. Heat spread through her body at an alarming rate. Her clit pulsed and her pussy clenched. His mouth was creating such delicious sensations.

"Zoey," he whispered, his cool breath caressing her skin. "Look down, baby. See what I see."

She lowered her head and let out a gasp. The rope was tied above and below her breasts, squeezing them, but also making them fuller. Her nipples were hard like little berries.

The heat and desire in his eyes made her skin tingle with pleasure and need. "I want you," she whispered.

A grin blossomed over his lips. He stood and put his arms around her back. Within minutes her wrists were free, and then her breasts. His fingers massaged her arms before he picked her up and carried her to the bed.

He threw back the comforter and gently set her down. He took off her shoes and socks and unfastened her pants. "How did shibari make you feel?" His fingers slid beneath the fabric. She lifted her hips so he could strip off her pants.

"Hot," she whispered.

Khalid laughed. "Your body is so pliant right now." He tossed her pants and underwear aside.

Zoey shifted on the cool sheets. She was naked and he was still dressed, yet she wasn't cold. No, the heat coming from his eyes was keeping her warm. She held her arms out to him. She wanted his skin against hers. His body on hers.

"Soon." He skimmed his hands over her legs as he pushed them apart and knelt between them. "First I get to feast."

Before she could react, his fingers were parting her nether lips and his mouth covered her mound. At the first flick of his tongue her hips bucked. "Khalid." His tongue swept up and down over her clit, creating delicious sensations throughout her body.

"You taste like honey." His voice was husky.

"I need you," she whispered, as her fingers grasped at his shoulders.

He gave a sharp nod. Khalid stripped out of his pants and reached for the nightstand. Zoey grasped his hand in hers. "I'm safe, and I'm on the pill." Her breath caught at her first sight of him. Damn, the man was built.

Khalid entwined his fingers with hers as he moved over her body. He took her hands over her head and pressed them against the mattress. He shifted his hips. The tip of his cock brushed her entrance.

He shifted his hips. "Yes," she whispered, her fingers tightening on his as his cock pushed in. Her pussy stretched with his entrance.

"So tight."

"It's been a while." Her breathing rushed out of her as he surged into her. "Damn."

His lips brushed her forehead. "Zoey?"

"I'm good. You're just so ... big."

"I think you're exaggerating." He pulled back and then thrust back in.

"Right." She panted as he began moving faster. "Oh, yes, Khalid." Her toes began to tingle, and that feeling moved up her legs and spread through her body. She wasn't going to last long; it had been too long.

He rotated his hips, and his cock rubbed her G-spot. "Fuck." Her pussy tightened as her climax rolled through her.

"That's it, baby. Come for me. Let me feel you." He kept thrusting.

Zoey didn't think she could take much more as she began to float down from her orgasm, but another started to build.

Khalid thrust hard, and he began to pulse inside her, trigging another climax.

He rolled them to their side, still connected as the aftershocks flowed through both of their bodies, their harsh breathing filling the room.

She tried to gather her scrambled thoughts, but instead, she kissed his cheek and whispered, "That was fantastic," before her lashes fell.

Khalid grinned as Zoey fell asleep. He'd worn her out. That wasn't a bad thing. He shifted, pulling himself from her willing body. Lord, this woman disarmed him like no other.

He went into the bathroom and cleaned up, then came back with a warm washcloth and cleaned Zoey up. Once that was done, he grabbed the comforter and climbed into bed.

When he put his arm around Zoey, she cuddled right up to him, and he pulled the comforter over both of them. She most definitely was getting under his skin, and he didn't mind it at all. Now he just had to keep her safe.

❧ *9* ☙

Zoey found Catherine, Sara, and Bobbie in the dining room the next morning. Khalid had woken her with a kiss before leaving to meet with Ryan. She'd snuggled into his warm spot for a while, then got up. She had a long list of things to do today.

"Oh, good, Zoey, you're here," Catherine said. "Come sit down."

She grabbed a cup of coffee and then took a seat next to Catherine. "What's going on?"

"Here." Sara handed her a piece of paper.

Zoey looked at it. "Ah, the top ten events for the anniversary party."

"Yep," Bobbie said. "We're going to figure out which ones we'll each attend."

"I'm not part of the royal family." She really wasn't.

"Really?" Sara's eyes twinkled with mischief. "You are as much family as the rest of us. Plus I noticed Khalid leading you into his room last night. Is it getting serious between you two?"

Zoey closed her eyes as her cheeks heated. Damn, she'd hoped no one had seen them. What could she say? It was the truth. Part of her wanted to be part of the family.

"Quit teasing. Good for the two of you," Catherine said. "Besides, anyone can see you and Khalid are a couple, and therefore you are most definitely part of the family. So let's go through this list."

Zoey wanted to protest, but the happiness in Catherine's eyes stopped her. Maybe being a part of the family, at least for a short time, wouldn't be so bad. She hoped they'd understand when she left for her next job.

For the next two hours, the women ate, drank, and discussed the list until they'd figured out who would go to which events. "I'll get this to Khalid, so he and the guys can go over all the security procedures."

Zoey's stomach fluttered. "Catherine, I'll need to go shopping. I don't travel with fancy clothes, so I don't have anything with me."

"Oh, that's no problem. I'll take you to the marketplace to see Ramala. She'll get you fixed up in no time," Catherine said.

"We should all go," Sara said.

Bobbie groaned. "I guess so." Bobbie grinned at Zoey. "I hate getting dressed up. I'm more a jeans and T-shirt kind of gal."

"And I'm a khakis, T-shirt, and hiking boots type." Zoey laughed.

"That's settled. I'll let Malik know we need to go see Ramala, so he can talk with Khalid and arrange it. This afternoon, if we can. The first event starts next Monday."

Zoey fell onto her bed at six. Dinner was in an hour. She just wanted to curl up and go to sleep. Shopping with Catherine and Sara had been an experience. At least she hadn't been alone in that. Even Bobbie seemed a little overwhelmed at times.

Rolling to her feet, Zoey went into the bathroom and turned on the shower, stripped out of her clothes, and got under the hot water. Oh, that felt so good. She'd been enfolded in material, measurements had been taken, colors had been discussed. Zoey had explained that she was more comfortable in pants than dresses, but Ramala had assured her anything that was made for her would be comfortable.

All of them were to return to Ramala's in two days for a fitting so any adjustments could be made.

The shower door was pushed open, and Zoey opened her mouth to scream when Khalid stepped in.

"You scared me." She slapped his shoulder.

"I knocked, but you didn't answer." He pulled her wet body against his. "I came in, heard the shower, and thought I'd join you."

Her bones melted. "I'm glad you did. I missed you." She wiggled against his growing erection.

"Behave, woman." He pinched her nipple, making her squeal. "Dinner is soon, but I couldn't wait another minute to have you in my arms."

Zoey sighed and turned in his embrace. This strong, handsome man was doing things to her insides that no other had accomplished. She went up on her toes and brushed her lips against his. "Later, then," she whispered before he captured her mouth in a deep, hard kiss. If she wasn't careful she was going to fall in love with this man, and she couldn't do that. She had her job and her freedom to consider. And soon. But not tonight. Not right now. She gave herself up to the sensations coursing through her.

The next few days passed in relative quiet. The outfits Ramala had made were fabulous. Even Zoey had to admit the long dresses she'd made were comfortable. Plus, Ramala had made some very light pant-slips that could be worn under the dresses after Zoey's comment about being uncomfortable in that attire.

Each day, the brothers met with Khalid's security team, going over the events, all the plans, etc. They included the women's bodyguards, so during this time the women were confined to the palace. While they complained, they were good-natured about it.

Khalid had taken her aside and apologized about her having to curtail some of her time in town. Zoey told him she understood. He was trying to protect her and the others, but when they weren't under house arrest, she wanted to go out.

Khalid grinned and told her, "Of course." So Habib took her into Bashir City to work. And after she had requested it, with Khalid's approval, she was taken to the villages just outside the city limits, so she could talk to the people about the anniversary and take pictures.

Zoey already had enough material for ten more articles. She was learning so much about what Bashir had to offer. While the country did have oil, it also had crops of wheat and cotton, fruit and nut trees, sheep and cattle. It was a very well-rounded country. It helped that each region was able to concentrate on a different product.

The people she'd met loved working the land, and skills were often passed from father to son and mother to daughter. She loved listening to them talk, telling stories about their families. There was obvious pride.

Occasionally she would ask one of the older men about Kalif and how he felt about what was happening. The men called Kalif a traitor and hoped he would be gone soon. Several of the men spoke with the security team that accompanied Zoey.

Zoey stood up from the makeshift workstation in her room and stretched. She'd just finished another article. Tomorrow, she'd sort out the pictures.

On Monday, the anniversary celebration would begin. Malik and Catherine were attending the first event that night, more or less like an opening ceremony. Khalid would be there with the security team.

A knock on her door brought her out of her musings. She opened the door to see Khalid standing there. "Hi, sweetheart." He leaned down and kissed her.

Since the night they'd done shibari and first had sex, he'd been more open with her. Kissing her, sharing showers, sleeping together, and just being with each other.

"Hi, I wasn't expecting to see you until later," she said, closing the door after he entered her room.

"Everything is under control, and I was ordered to take some time off."

Zoey laughed. "Like you follow orders."

"In this case, yes. I've missed you." He pulled her into his arms and kissed her again.

Zoey melted against him. "I've missed you too," she said after he broke the kiss.

"I thought since all the craziness would start on Monday, maybe tonight we'd have dinner in my room and enjoy some private time together."

She smiled. "I'd love that. What are you planning?"

"A surprise. Come to my room at six." He brushed another kiss over her lips before releasing her. "Just wear the robe I put in your closet and nothing else." With those words he opened the door and left.

Robe? What robe? Zoey walked over to the closet and looked inside. Yep, hanging there was a beautiful forest-green robe. With a giggle, Zoey went and shut down her computer.

She wanted to take a quick shower and shave her legs to get ready for her night with Khalid.

Khalid checked everything in his room once again. Why was he so nervous? They'd already done shibari together and made love, but tonight he wanted to take her higher.

His ropes were all laid out, along with several toys and something he'd made for her earlier. A knock on the door had him taking a deep breath before crossing the room to open the door.

Zoey stood there, her eyes bright. "Umm ... let me in." She pushed at his chest, and he fell back a step as she swept past him. This wasn't like her.

"Is everything all right?" he asked, closing the door.

"Yes. I didn't want anyone to see me."

He frowned. Was she having second thoughts about them? He stared at her face. It didn't seem like it. She had an excited glow to her. "Why?"

"Why what?" She turned and looked at the room. "This is nice."

He'd dimmed the lights, and dinner was on the side table waiting for them. But first he wanted to get to the bottom of her worry about someone seeing her. "Why didn't you want someone seeing you?" He took her by the shoulders and turned her so she faced him once again.

"Because I'm naked under my robe. It's embarrassing." Her cheeks turned pink, and he fought a smile. "Privacy matters to me."

His confident, spunky Zoey was afraid of someone seeing her enter his room? It wasn't as if his family and bodyguards didn't know what was going on. But he wouldn't tell her that.

Malik had ordered him to take the night off. They all would, because they wanted to spend some quiet time with their women before the craziness of the anniversary party started.

"I don't like that smirky smile playing around your lips," she said running her fingers over his chest. He had on only a pair of black cotton pants.

"I hate to break it to you, sweetheart, but nothing in the palace is ever private."

Her eyes widened. "You mean they know about … ?" She waved her hand toward his ropes.

"That? No. But you being in my room, yes." He rubbed her nose with his. "Let's eat, then we can have some fun." He led her over to the table and held her chair out for her; once she was seated, he took the lid off her plate.

"Lamb stew."

"One of your favorites." He took his seat and watched her tear off a piece of bread and dip it into the stew. He loved how she enjoyed her food.

They talked about the upcoming parties and the parade as they ate. Khalid found he really enjoyed talking things over with Zoey. She had a quick mind, and sometimes saw things he didn't.

"Is there something on your mind?" he asked, after putting the empty dishes back on the small cart. While she'd been talkative over dinner, something told him she was holding something back.

"A little something." Her fingers drew circles on the tabletop, something she did when she was nervous.

"What is it?" He kept his voice soft.

"I … " She blew out a breath. "Khalid, are we in a relationship?"

He was surprised by her question. It was obvious to him. "Yes, is there a reason you don't want to be?" His gut clenched. Was she just in this for the sex?

"Yes and no." She lifted her head, and the confusion in her silver eyes tugged at him. "I feel something for you, it's more than lust, but you know once my job is done here, I'll be leaving."

"Is that what you're worried about? What will happen when you leave?"

"A little bit." She reached across the small table and touched his cheek. "You're a caring man, and I don't want to hurt you."

He started to say she couldn't hurt him, but the words never formed. He was already attached to her. Khalid didn't want to frighten her. "Why don't we cross that road when we get to it?"

She nodded. "It's more than sex for me. I just wanted you to know that."

His heart swelled. They were close to being on the same page, but he wouldn't push her. Not right now. "It's more than that for me as well." He stood and drew her from her chair and led her to the middle of the sitting room. He'd set up a chair and his equipment. "Tonight I'd like to do something different and special."

"Yes, Sir."

His cock pulsed at her words. She fell right into the D/s role naturally. He undid the tie on her robe and slipped it from her shoulders. He'd turned down the air conditioning in his room earlier so she wouldn't be cold. Tossing her robe over the sofa, he picked up the piece of rope he'd worked on earlier.

"What is that?" she asked when he turned around with it in his hands.

"Something special for you." He knelt. "Lift your right foot, then your left." He placed the rope around her ankles, then began to maneuver it up over her calves and thighs. "You see, I made you rope underwear."

The fit was good around her waist. He checked her legs, and it was good there as well. She shifted from one foot to the other, and a shiver went through her. "Ah, is it supposed to ... rub me down there?"

Khalid stood and smiled. "It can be part of the stimulation, but tonight I have something else in mind." He turned, picked up one of his toys, and knelt down. "Spread your legs, sweetheart."

He was pleased when she did as he asked with no hesitation. He valued her trust in him. He took the small bullet, inserted it in the small pocket he had made, and then stood.

Zoey shifted from one foot to the other some more. Her skin was flushed, so that was a good sign. "Tonight you're going to sit on the chair, and I'm going to tie you to it."

"Agreeable, Sir."

He nodded, then guided her to the chair. Once she was seated, her spread her legs. "I'm going to tie your legs and then your arms."

"Yes, Sir."

Khalid picked up the rope he needed. His mind centered itself on his task. He sat on the floor and positioned her right foot slightly to the side of the chair. Taking the folded rope, he loosely wrapped it around the inside and outside of her ankle, then pulled the rope over the other end, did it again, and then created a knot. He did the same with her left ankle.

He looped the rope around the back of the chair on both sides and stood. With a gentle touch, he grasped her right arm and positioned it. He made sure her shoulders were centered and level with the top of the chair. He wrapped the loose ends of the rope around her wrist and carefully tightened it, but made sure it didn't cut off her circulation. Then he did her left arm.

Once finished, he checked the tightness of the rope before tying the rest off so her arms were pulled slightly behind her. Khalid strode around Zoey, checking his work. Her breathing was a little rapid, but her skin had a nice tone to it.

"How are you feeling?"

"Vulnerable, Sir."

He was pleased with her honesty. The way he had her tied, her body was open to whatever he wanted. "If anything starts to go numb or tingle, let me know right away."

"Yes, Sir."

Khalid bent down until he could see into those beautiful eyes of hers. "Do you trust me, sweetheart?"

She smiled. "I wouldn't let you tie me up if I didn't, Sir."

"Cheeky." He brushed a kiss over her lips as he straightened and went over to the sofa. He picked up what he wanted and moved behind her. "I made this little item while waiting for you." He dangled the rope blindfold in front of her.

She inhaled. "That is beautiful, Sir."

"It's a prosperity knot, basically pulling the rope around and through." He settled the blindfold over her eyes. She sucked in a breath. Khalid carefully tied it, making sure not to catch her hair in the knot. "Okay?"

"Yes, Sir." Her voice was a little shaky.

He smoothed his hands over her shoulders and down her arms until he reached her hands. He put his finger inside her hand. "Squeeze." She did. Good, no issues with the tie. She relaxed her hand, and he slid his finger out and picked up the small remote on the table.

He flipped on the first button. Zoey jumped and let out a small cry as the toy against her clit came to life.

"Do you like my toy?"

Zoey pursed her lips together, and he let out a chuckle. He set the remote aside as the bullet buzzed against her clit, then smoothed his palms over her collarbone until he could cup her breasts.

"Pretty breasts with nice rosy nipples." He flicked them with his thumbs as Zoey tried to wiggle in her bonds. He pinched her nipples, and she let out a cry. "Nice and hard now."

Zoey fought not to voice her opinion of what Khalid was doing to her, because damn it, he was arousing her beyond endurance. The bullet vibrating against her clit was bad enough, but now he was playing with her breasts.

Hell, already while he'd been tying her up, her body had heated excitement flowing through her veins. Being restrained and at his mercy flipped a switch in her. In a way it surprised her. She'd never been this compliant with a man, but Khalid was different.

He was all about protection. His family, her, his security officers. Over the past few weeks she'd seen him in action. Even when they'd played a few nights ago, like tonight, he checked in with her and made sure she was comfortable.

Well, as comfortable as she could be with her body being so aroused. She tried to shift her hips to put more pressure on her clit, but she couldn't.

"Oh, do you want more?" His words were soft against her ear. The vibrations on the toy went up.

A shudder went through her body. Her breathing hiccupped. "Sir?"

"Yes, love." The endearment had her heart skipping a beat. His lips covered her right breast, and any thoughts flew out of her mind. Her head fell back as he licked and bit her nipple. So many sensations.

Without her sight she couldn't see what he was doing. Hearing wasn't doing her much good either, since he moved like a panther. Smell? She inhaled. Her muscles relaxed further as she inhaled sandalwood and citrus, Khalid's unique scent. She couldn't touch him, as she was tied up. But damn, she wanted to press her nose to his skin and drown in his scent.

"Did you have a question, love?"

She shook her head as her nipple tightened more in the cool air of the room. But she wasn't cold. Then she realized he was blowing on her nipple. She was so overheated his breath felt cool.

A tingling started in her toes, and she wasn't sure if it was because her feet were going to sleep or her impending climax. But she had promised to tell him.

"Sir, my toes are tingling."

Instantly, his hands were on her feet, rubbing them. "They're not cold to the touch. Can you wiggle your toes?"

Zoey tried, but when she did, the tingling shot up her leg, making her jump. Khalid swore, and the sounds of him moving swiftly reached her ears. The next thing she knew, the bullet was turned off, the rope around her hands was pulled loose, and then the one around her feet was loose too.

His hands began flexing her left foot and then her right in gentle motions. The tingling stopped. "Better?"

"Yes, Sir. I'm sorry." Tears gathered behind her eyelids and leaked out around the rope blindfold.

"Sweetheart." The blindfold was removed, and he pulled her into his arms. "Shhhh, are you hurt?"

Zoey shook her head.

"Then what is causing the tears?"

"I didn't want you to stop." She was lifted, carried into his bedroom, and placed on his bed.

"Zoey, sweetie. Open your eyes and look at me."

While his voice was soft and coaxing, there was an order behind the words. Zoey could do nothing but obey. She blinked a few times to bring her eyes back into focus, to see a concerned Khalid leaning over her.

"Never ever worry about asking me to stop." He brushed the tears off her cheeks with his fingers. "Your wellbeing is of upmost importance."

"But," she began.

"No buts." He traced his fingers over her lips. "You did exactly as I asked you to do. No more tears."

"But I ruined it." He didn't understand. She'd made him stop, ruined his enjoyment of seeing her tied up.

"Zoey." Khalid let out a sigh and pressed against her. "Does that feel like you ruined anything?"

His hard cock pressed against her outside thigh. "Oh."

"Oh is right." He kissed her cheek. "I'm going to go turn out the lights. I'll be right back."

She nodded and watched him leave, enjoying the way the pants molded to his tight ass. She didn't ruin it for him. Good. She shifted on the sheets and realized she still wore the rope panties and the bullet was still in place. It came to life as she finished the thought, and her hands went to her mound.

"Do not touch it." Khalid's order had her turning her head toward the door. He stood there watching her.

"You're teasing me again," she said. Not that she minded, but damn it, the toy wasn't doing much but putting her on edge.

"Yes. Mine to tease. Mine to play with. Mine to love." He said the words with each step he took toward the bed. Her heart pounded. His words spun in her brain, but she only focused on one: 'mine.' It hit her. She was his. Once by the side, he set the small remote on the table, and stripped off his pants.

His hard cock sprang free, and Zoey licked her lips. Would he let her? "I want to suck you."

He stiffened, then relaxed. Had she surprised him by the request? Maybe, but she wanted to taste him. She couldn't wait to feel him between her lips. She wasn't going to give him a chance to say no.

Zoey slipped off the bed, grabbed a pillow, and then pushed him until he was seated at the edge of the mattress. She put the pillow on the floor, pushed his legs apart, and knelt.

She gripped the base of his cock. The head was already glistening with his desire. She leaned down and gave it a lick.

"Sweetheart." He said the word with a groan as she enveloped him in her mouth.

He was hot and hard. She licked and sucked, enjoying the feel of him not only in her mouth, but in her hand as well. When the bullet against her clit sped up, she yelped around his cock.

Two could play that game. She let her fingers slide from his base to his balls, rolling them gently between her fingers, before slipping down and finding that sweet spot on a man.

"Fuck," he roared, almost coming off the bed. The bullet stopped vibrating, and his cock was pulled from her mouth. She started to ask him what was going on when she was lifted, thrown onto the mattress.

The rope panties were pulled off of her, the bullet was removed, and he was poised over her. His cock brushed her entrance. "I can't wait," he said, as he slammed into her.

Zoey accepted him with open arms. She'd gotten to him. Broken his control. Part of her was amazed she could do that, while another wondered just how far she could push him. Her hand caressed his ass and moved lower.

"Don't even think it," he growled against her lips. "Bad girls get a spanking."

"Maybe I want one." Oh, she was really poking the sleeping cat now.

His eyes narrowed. "Later." His lips captured hers as he pumped into her.

Zoey closed her eyes and let his brand of loving carry her away.

～

The next morning, Khalid looked down at a sleeping Zoey, and his heart swelled. He was falling in love with this woman. Somehow, she'd wormed her way past all his defenses. Not that it bothered him. Zoey fit in with his life.

She didn't make demands on his time, and when they were together, it was explosive. As much as he didn't like her going out and taking pictures and talking with the people, in case Kalif got wind of it, he let her go. He loved her even more because she understood and did her best to fall in with his protection.

Her respect for the people of Bashir was evident, but she also had a way of getting the people to talk. Habib had told him about it when they met to discuss keeping Zoey safe. Knowing how she felt about her overprotective parents, Khalid tried hard not to cross that invisible line.

Because of Zoey's work and her discussions with the people, they'd found out Kalif was trying to recruit more men, mainly by threatening the villages. But the villagers so far had stood up to him, and he'd retreated.

The villagers were also reporting when these things happened, if not to Zoey and Habib, then to security. This gave them precious intel on Kalif, and Kalif's circle seemed to be getting smaller and smaller.

Zoey shifted, and Khalid glanced down at her to see her lashes raise and her beautiful silver eyes appear.

"I don't think I've ever seen anyone with silver eyes."

"It's rare, but it happens when the pigmentation doesn't form right."

"They're beautiful, just like you." He brushed a kiss over her lips, but pulled back when she would have deepened it. "I need to get dressed and go with Ryan to the first event venue. We want to be sure everything is as we were told."

"I understand."

Khalid rolled out of bed. "But that doesn't mean we can't shower together."

Zoey laughed, climbed out of bed, and ran for the shower. He followed her with a big grin on his face.

~

"Lord, I'm nervous." It was Tuesday evening and the first event she and Khalid were attending as a couple.

"You'll be fine," Sara said, helping her into the dress from Ramala.

Zoey looked at herself in the mirror. The aquamarine dress had threads of gold running through it, and if Zoey turned just right, it sparkled in the light.

"Thank you for helping me." Zoey turned to Sara. "I've never really had girlfriends, and all of you welcomed me into the fold without question."

Sara laughed. "Of course we did, we all know how it is to date royalty."

Zoey nodded. She wasn't going to argue with Sara. Everyone wanted to believe she and Khalid were a couple. In a way, they were, but she also knew that as soon as the anniversary celebrations were over, she'd need to move on to her next job.

Her shoulders dropped and a heaviness settled in her chest. She didn't want to leave Bashir. Hell, she didn't want to leave Khalid, but part of her feared she'd grow bored with all the restrictions.

Sara adjusted the back of the dress. "Perfect, just slip on your shoes, and you're ready to go."

Zoey slipped on the flat shoes, and there was a knock on the door. Sara walked over and opened the door. Zoey turned, and she had to fight not to gape at Khalid. He was dressed in black pants, tucked into high-polished black boots.

He wore a white tunic with red and gold running through it. A sash made up of red and gold finished the outfit, and he looked deliciously handsome. A sword in a scabbard hung at his side.

"He cleans up well, doesn't he?" Sara commented.

"You can say that again." Zoey held her breath as Khalid walked up to her.

"Good evening, my beautiful Zoey." He leaned down and brushed a kiss against her lips. "You look ... I wish I spoke as many languages as you do so I could say how divine you look."

Zoey's cheeks turned hot, but she smiled at him. "You look more than handsome, I'll have to beat the women off with a stick."

"Good thing I have my sword with me because I'll be fighting for your hand."

Sara let out a laugh. "Stop the flirting you two, or you'll be late."

"Yes, Lady Sara." Khalid bowed to Sara, then drew Zoey's hand to the crook of his arm and led her down the stairs. Habib and Ryan stood there waiting for them, both in dress uniforms, which consisted of red and gold.

"I have several men already at the venue," Ryan said.

Khalid nodded, and they went out to the SUV.

Zoey tried to quell her nerves as the vehicle pulled up in front of the venue. Press and people were lined up behind rope. There was even a red carpet. Khalid emerged first, and the crowd went wild.

He reached back and helped her out of the vehicle. The crowd went silent for a moment, then burst out in cheers. Camera flashes went off, almost blinding her. Khalid tucked her arm into his and led her up the walkway into the building.

She breathed a sigh of relief when they made their way into the foyer. Her nerves were dancing an Irish jig inside her body. Maybe she shouldn't have allowed herself to be talked into this.

A man in what looked like a butler's outfit grinned when he saw Khalid. "Your Highness." He nodded to the other two men standing inside the doors. The man stepped through, and Khalid followed.

"His Royal Highness Prince Khalid and Lady Zoey," he announced in a loud clear voice. All eyes turned to them, and Zoey wanted to sink into the floor.

"Smile," Khalid whispered, and she found herself obeying as he led her into the room.

Everyone was dressed to the nines, and she wasn't comfortable in situations like this. She was more of a hang out with the guys and gals at the local bar drinking beer type than someone who'd attend a big fancy party.

But she kept her head high and smiled as they walked. Khalid stopped and introduced her to person after person. Zoey's head spun with all the names. She'd never remember them all.

When music started playing, Khalid swung her into his arms and onto the dance floor. Zoey was grateful she'd taken dance lessons a few years ago for a coworker's wedding.

"I'm never going to remember all those names," she whispered.

"It will come in time," Khalid said.

Zoey sighed and relaxed into his embrace. Tonight wasn't for thinking about how little time she had left in Bashir and with Khalid. She wanted to enjoy the time she had with him and being in his arms tonight was very enjoyable.

When the music stopped, Khalid took her over to the buffet table. "Why don't you pick out a plate full, and I'll go get us something to drink?"

"All right." She watched him walk away, observing how all the women's gazes followed him. She filled a plate, and then found a small table away from the dance floor for the two of them. She hoped Khalid would see her, as there was a big potted plant next to her.

"Did you see her?" A woman's voice carried past the plant.

"Yes. She doesn't belong," another woman said.

Zoey nibbled at a cracker. Who were these women talking about, and why were women so catty?

"Another foreigner with her sights on the last bachelor prince. Khalid can do better than her."

She almost choked on her food. They were talking about her.

"And that outfit."

"One of Ramala's. I don't know why the queen uses her. Her clothing is old-fashioned and ugly."

Zoey glanced down at her dress. It wasn't ugly. In fact, it looked damn good on her. But it didn't stop feelings of inadequacy from raising their ugly head. Stop, she ordered herself. She wouldn't allow them to pull this crap. If they did this to her, what about other women in the country?

"I wonder how she garnered his attention. I heard she's a photographer or something."

"He's probably keeping an eye on her so she doesn't do something embarrassing."

Like hell. Zoey rose to her feet to see Khalid standing there, his face furious. She shook her head and rounded the plant.

The three women looked up, their faces going pale. "Umm, Lady Zoey," one blurted out. This was the one who'd said she was a foreigner.

"Excuse us, Lady Zoey," the other one said. This was the first one who'd talked.

"You are not excused." Zoey allowed her gaze to sweep up and down each woman. "Please don't let me stop your little critique session."

"We were just talking, Lady Zoey," the third one said in a quiet voice.

"Now it's Lady Zoey instead of that foreigner." Zoey shook her head. One thing she couldn't stand was the cattiness of other women. "Is your clothing so tight it cut off the blood to your brains?" The women stayed silent, but their gazes wouldn't meet hers. "For your information, Ramala's dresses are not ugly, and I'm proud to be wearing one of her creations. I'm a travel blogger and journalist, not just some photographer." The room had gone silent, but Zoey didn't stop. "As for embarrassing. I think you three accomplished that all on your own."

"They have," Khalid said, coming up behind her and putting his arms around her waist.

The host of the party, whose name Zoey couldn't remember, came bustling up. "Prince Khalid, Lady Zoey, I am so sorry."

Zoey turned to him and smiled. "You have nothing to apologize for. The party is lovely."

The host waved his hand, and two men came over. "Please escort the women out."

"But Saleem," one woman started.

"No. I will not have such disgraceful women at this celebration." The women were escorted away. Saleem raised his hands, and the music started once again as people resumed talking. "My apologies again, Lady Zoey." He took her hand and kissed the back of it. "The people of Bashir think highly of you." Then he turned and left.

Zoey's face was hot when Khalid led her back to the table. "I'm sorry," she whispered, trying to control the small tremors inside her. Confronting those women had been hard, but dang it, she couldn't let their comments slide.

"Zoey." Khalid slipped his arm around her shoulders.

"I should probably leave."

"No." His voice was adamant. "Look around the room, Zoey. What do you see?"

She forced herself to turn her head. "Everyone is dancing." She fully expected everyone to be staring at her and whispering.

"Yes, they are." There was a hint of laughter in his voice. "Saleem wasn't kidding when he said the people of Bashir love you."

"He said they think highly of me," she corrected.

"They love you." He squeezed her shoulders. "You've been out among them, helping them, talking to them. They are well aware those three women have never done a day of work in their lives. You've gained our country's respect and love by being you. Never stop."

His words brought a flush of pleasure and made her heart swell. "Really?"

"Yes, now eat something. I want to dance so I can hold you in my arms."

Zoey yawned as she filled her coffee cup the next morning. While the party had broken up around eleven, Khalid had brought her back to his room, and they had made love half the night. But the words of those women still bounced around in her brain, as did Khalid's words.

She had never felt at home as much she did here in Bashir. She was going to be sad to leave. Zoey shook her head and pushed her negative thoughts aside. She needed to make some headway on the pictures she'd been taking. She usually kept up nightly with them, but between the party, stuff going on at the palace, Khalid, and other things, she'd gotten behind.

The sun was out, and Zoey didn't want to be cooped up inside. She ran upstairs, grabbed her laptop, and made her way into the garden.

Catherine had told her she'd been working to make the garden more enjoyable by adding benches, tables, and chairs.

Zoey found one of the sets of tables and chairs, and sat down with her laptop. The air was crisp and clean. At least she had a full charge on her laptop, plus she had her external battery, so she could spend several hours out here. She opened her photo gallery and began going through and sorting the pictures.

~

"Zoey." Bobbie's soft touch on her shoulder made Zoey jump and turn her head.

"Hey, Bobbie." Zoey sat back and groaned as her back protested. "How long were you standing there?"

"A couple of minutes; you were totally lost in your work."

"Yeah." Zoey looked at the clock on her computer. "Yikes, I've been at this for hours." It was so easy for her to lose herself in her work. She usually set an alarm but today she wasn't worried about time.

"Habib mentioned you were out here. I thought maybe you'd like to share lunch." Bobbie lifted the small basket she carried and put it on the table.

"You are a saint."

Bobbie laughed. "Don't tell Rafi that. He likes my bad parts."

Zoey closed her laptop and pushed it to the side as Bobbie unloaded the basket with chicken sandwiches, chips, and fruit juice. "And for dessert," Bobbie said pulling out a container with a flourish. "Chocolate chip cookies."

"Oh, my God, give me." Zoey held out her hand. She hadn't had a good chocolate chip cookie in a while.

Bobbie laughed and handed Zoey the container. Zoey opened it and the bliss of their scent had her groaning. Then she shut the lid and set them aside. "I better eat real food first, or I'll eat all those cookies."

"You have to share," Bobbie said with a laugh.

The two talked and laughed as they ate. Bobbie shared tidbits about being part of the royal family, and Zoey shared about her work and her life.

"I had another reason for this impromptu lunch," Bobbie said.

"Oh." Zoey popped another chocolate chip cookie into her mouth. At this rate, she was going to gain ten pounds if she wasn't careful.

"We heard about the women at last night's party."

Zoey's enjoyment of the cookies fled. She closed the container and took a deep breath. "Are Catherine and Malik upset?"

Bobbie laughed. "Oh, hell no." Bobbie reached across the table and patted Zoey's hand. "Zoey, you did the right thing in calling them out. Catherine was so appreciative of your standing up for Ramala's creations."

"They're beautiful clothes. Those women were just being catty, and I can't stand that."

"Most of us can't, but Catherine, as queen, has to be a little more circumspect. These three apparently have harassed her at a couple of events as well."

"Oh, no. Have I made things worse?" Zoey bit her lower lip. It was the last thing she wanted to do to Catherine or the other women who made her feel so welcome.

"Actually, you made things a lot better."

"How?"

"Word has been circulating about them and what they said last night and how you confronted them. There have been calls and letters all day advising that the women have been disinvited to the anniversary parties."

"Oh, no, that will just make things worse." These women would be angry at her and the family. This wasn't good.

Bobbie shook her head. "Zoey, you take on too much. These women are from good Bashir families. Those families are very embarrassed. You see, Bashir children are raised to embrace differences, to look beyond the color of one's skin, how much money people have, all those things. Yes, there is still work to be done, but as a whole, Bashir is a very tolerant country."

"How did the country become so tolerant?" Zoey was curious, but also this would help her articles. She really needed to get to reading those books she'd bought on Bashir history.

"From what I know, the brothers' grandfather wasn't very modern, but he believed in equality. When their dad took over, he took it a step further. Making sure every child was educated and teaching them about the world, not just their own country."

"I forgot you're a teacher."

"Yes. Right now I'm just teaching Zain, but I want to teach at one of the schools eventually." Bobbie shook her head. "Malik is continuing like his father to make sure Bashir survives as a country."

"That's great, but it still doesn't mean those women won't want to get even."

Bobbie laughed. "Trust me when I say they won't. They're going to be upset, yes, but they'll learn their lesson. And if you happen to run into them again, they'll be very polite."

"If you say so."

"I do. Can I see what you were working on?"

"Sure." Zoey showed Bobbie some of her photos. As they were going through them, she noticed that in a series of photos she took, the same man was in the background. When Bobbie left to go help Rafi in the stables, Zoey went through the series again. There were thirty, all with this man in them.

A shiver slid up her spine. There was something about him. A vibe she got even through the photos. Shutting her laptop, she grabbed her stuff and went to find Khalid. She found him in Malik's office.

"Do you two have a minute?" she asked. She didn't want to disturb them if they were in the middle of something important.

"Come on in, Zoey. You're a far better sight than my brother," Malik said.

"The same could be said for you." Khalid brushed a kiss over her cheek when she sat down. "Is there something wrong?"

"Yes and no." Zoey set her computer on Malik's desk and opened it up. "Bobbie and I had lunch together. I was showing her my photos when I noticed the same man showing up in them." She brought up the photos as Malik rounded his desk to look.

Both men swore as they looked at the photos. "That's Kalif," Malik said.

"He's in Bashir City, and we didn't know it." Khalid drew his hand through his short black hair. "How did I miss this?"

"Khalid," Malik started.

"No, Malik. It's my job."

"Khalid," Zoey said softly. She waited until she had his attention. "Look at these pictures. He's not making himself known. He's staying in the shadows, and not making it obvious that he's there." Zoey didn't want Khalid to beat himself up over this. "He's leaning against the building like he's just a normal everyday guy."

"But he's not," Khalid said.

"No, but he's not doing anything to make anyone suspicious or to make himself stand out," Zoey pointed out.

"Zoey's right," Malik said. "Can you go through the pictures again?"

"Sure."

They went through the pictures one by one, three more times. "It's obvious he was waiting for someone," Malik said.

"Someone who didn't show up." Khalid rubbed his chin. "Zoey, when did you take these?"

Zoey went to her file directory. "Three days ago. I'm behind on going through my photos."

"Do not blame yourself," Malik said. "It's amazing you even found this."

"Yes, whatever Kalif is up to, at least we know his contact didn't show up," Khalid said.

Zoey nodded. "If you see anything more in the photos, let us know," Malik said.

"Of course." She was being dismissed. Closing her laptop, she stood and cradled it in her arm. Khalid took her by the elbow and escorted her to the door.

"Thank you, Zoey," he whispered.

"You don't need to thank me."

"I do." He dipped his head and brushed his lips over hers. "Later we'll have some fun."

Her blood heated at his mention of fun. "I'd like that." She brushed her fingers over his cheek before stepping around him and out the door.

~

Khalid spent the next few hours in Malik's office with Ryan, strategizing about what Kalif might be doing in Bashir City and what they could do.

"The final parade is next week, and there's only one additional event the family is attending," Ryan said.

"True," Khalid said as he looked over the schedule.

"So Kalif is either going to try something at the parade or the last event," Malik said.

"We've got everything covered," Ryan said. "We'll have extra security at the event."

"The parade makes the most sense," Khalid said. "We'll have security there, but with the crowds and everything, we're not going to be able to cover it all."

"True, which is why I wanted to ask about bringing in a couple of sharpshooters," Ryan said.

Khalid stiffened and stared at Ryan.

"Yeah, I know, you've been resistant to the idea, but if Kalif does try something, at least we could possibly mitigate casualties," Ryan said.

"Or cause more," Khalid said.

"Khalid," Malik said. "What is the issue with sharpshooters? You're one yourself."

"Too many variables. The chances of an innocent person being hurt are too high." He should know.

"And you don't think the chances of people being hurt are high with Kalif?"

"Umm, excuse me," Ryan said, slipping from Malik's office.

"It's just too dangerous," Khalid said to his brother. The more people in the mix, the more dangerous. Especially with sharpshooters, things went wrong.

"Why is it too dangerous? I trust you and Ryan to pick the right men. Men who won't take chances if things get out of hand."

"There are things that can't be controlled." Khalid fought to keep his temper down. Malik didn't understand. Accidents happened. Innocent people died. He'd seen it, he'd been a part of it, and he would never forget it. Which was why he rarely used his sharpshooting skills in the field, only in practice to keep himself sharp.

"Is there something else?" Malik clasped his brother on the shoulder.

"It's nothing." He'd never told his family about what had happened during training with the UK special forces, and he never would. It was his burden to bear.

"I think Ryan's idea has merit." Malik stared at his brother. "I won't make it an order, but please look into it. I know you want to keep everyone safe."

Khalid nodded and left Malik's office to go find Ryan.

"I'm sorry, Khalid, I thought you would have discussed it," Ryan said.

He wanted to be angry with Ryan but couldn't. The man was the best at what he did, and he was only doing his job. "It's fine. Let's go over the men you picked out and see if we can make a decision."

Because regardless of whether he agreed or not, Malik was right. He wanted to keep everyone safe. A couple of sharpshooters at the parade would cover areas he wouldn't be able to.

"I need a night away from the palace and all the craziness," Catherine said three nights later.

Zoey grinned. Even she was getting a little stir-crazy. Since she had shown the pictures of Kalif to Malik and Khalid, they'd been even more restrictive on the women. She understood they wanted them safe, but something had to give. The last event had been held last night; now there was only the parade in two days.

"You and me both," Sara commented.

"Is there any reason we can't go out?" Zoey asked.

Bobbie laughed. "Four very stubborn brothers."

"They are just trying to keep us safe. We've been targets before," Catherine said.

"Yeah, but yours was a crazy minister, mine was a deranged brother, and Bobbie's ... well, that was directly tied to Kalif," Sara said.

"That's all true." Catherine let out a little laugh. "Seriously, I need a girls' night out."

"You know they are not going to allow that," Zoey said.

"True." Sara rubbed her forehead. "Honestly, our bodyguards take us out during the daytime. Maybe if we talk to our men and explain we really need this night out, they'll listen."

"If we can get Malik to say yes, he might be able to bring the rest of them around," Catherine said.

"Ladies, is this a good idea?" While Zoey was feeling hemmed in like the rest of them, security of the royal family had to come first.

"We can go to Wafi's," Bobbie said. "Our security knows that place inside and out. It's a family place; no one would bother us there."

Zoey shook her head. When these three got an idea into their heads ... She had to smile, though. They were their own women, strong fighters.

"Let's go face the lion in his den," Catherine said, jumping up and leading the way to Malik's office.

Malik frowned when he saw the four women enter his office. Zoey stayed off to the side, but Catherine marched up to her husband. "We need a girls' night out."

"No," Malik said, crossing his arms.

"Malik," Catherine started.

"No, sweetheart. It's too dangerous."

"Malik, we'll each have our bodyguards, and we only want to go to Wafi's restaurant. We'll be safe," Sara said.

"Wafi will see to it," Bobbie added.

Zoey could see Malik wavering. If they convinced him, then the other brothers would fall in line, all except Khalid. He wasn't going to risk the women's safety.

"Let me talk to my brothers. I'm making no promises."

Catherine's eyes sparkled. "Thank you." She kissed his cheek.

"I haven't said yes, yet."

"You're a reasonable man." Catherine led the women out of the office.

Zoey paced around her sitting room. It had been over an hour and nothing from the men. Was the silence a good thing or a bad thing? She was going crazy. A knock sounded on her door, and Khalid entered.

"I see you're as bad as my sisters-in-law. They're pacing as well."

"I'm sorry. I really don't want to make your job harder, nor do I want anyone to worry about any of us. It's ... " She shrugged her shoulders and kept pacing. She needed to work off this nervous energy.

"I agree with Catherine, you all need a night out."

Zoey stopped pacing and stared at Khalid. "You do?"

He laughed. "Yes. All of you will need to stay as normal as possible, and I'll make sure there are security provisions."

"Are you sure? I feel like this is a trivial matter."

"It's not." He crossed over to her and placed his hands on her shoulders. "I know being cooped up these last few days has been hard on you and the other women. And I suspect you're feeling a little trapped."

His insight melted her heart. "A bit. I'm used to coming and going as I please."

"I know." He lowered his forehead to rest on hers. "You have been in worse situations than this one, and I'm aware you can take care of yourself."

"You are a special man." She slipped her arms around his waist as a sheen of tears filled her eyes. He understood. Understood more than any other person in her life ever had.

"I do, but that doesn't mean there won't be some restrictions."

"Whatever you say." She grinned. "Wait. You got your brothers to agree?"

"I was the last holdout, and when I saw how the others were acting,

I knew something had to be done. Let's go downstairs while I brief everyone on the procedures that will take place."

~

"I can't believe they put trackers on us," Catherine commented when she and Zoey piled into the first SUV with their bodyguards. Sara and Bobbie were in the second SUV with their bodyguards.

"Me either." That had been a little bit of shock. Khalid explained they were new and this way they were able to keep track of the women. It was just a precaution, but it made all the men feel better about letting the women go out.

Zoey promised Khalid she'd stay safe and make sure the other women did too. She admired these women. They'd promised to behave themselves. Dinner and a few drinks at Wafi's, and then they'd be home.

Khalid had called Wafi, advising him of what was happening, and Wafi agreed to make sure the women would be safe in his establishment.

Wafi greeted them at the door. Habib and Hamaz stayed outside. Wafi took the women to a table, but Samir and Najah stood close to the entrance to the restaurant.

"I will have food and drink sent over. Please enjoy," Wafi said.

"I can't believe they let us go out," Bobbie said, popping a rice ball into her mouth.

"Me either," Sara commented.

"I think Zoey helped," Catherine said.

"I really didn't do anything." Zoey smiled at the women. "I think they realized we really needed to escape for a while."

"Maybe," Catherine said. "Malik commented that my pacing was making him nervous."

Sara laughed. "Hassan was ready to pull his hair out."

"Rafi threatened to take me over his knee if I didn't stop. I told him if he did then he'd be sleeping on the sofa for a month." Everyone laughed.

"It's just nice to get out of the palace without a formal function to go to," Catherine said.

"It is." Zoey had to agree.

The women toasted each other, ate, and drank some more. Wafi made sure they never ran out of fruit juice and food. When musicians came out to set up, Zoey wished she'd brought her camera.

She'd taken pictures a few weeks ago when Wafi's was closed, including some of the entertainers. Zoey frowned. These were different guys. Wafi had told her the musicians had been with him for years, and he never hired anyone else. The hair on the back of her neck stood up.

"Ladies, I suggest we make a quick trip to the bathroom before they start." The bathrooms were near the back. This way they didn't disturb the rest of the customers and didn't call attention to themselves. They could slip out the back door, Najah and Samir would follow.

"Sounds good." The women stood up.

As they made it to the hallway, a commotion had Zoey turning. Samir and Najah were fighting with three men, and the musicians were headed toward her and the other women.

"Damn," Zoey muttered. She hated when her instincts were right. "Catherine, Sara, Bobbie, out the back door and get back to the palace." Zoey pushed the three women toward the emergency exit as she turned to face the men.

She didn't know where Hamaz and Habib were, but she had confidence they would be there as soon as they could. Zoey would protect the other three women until they got away.

"Zoey," Catherine called.

"Go!" Zoey yelled. "Get to safety." She prepared herself. It wasn't going to be a fair fight, but she'd use everything she'd learned to give the women time to escape.

The first man came at her, and she slammed the palm of her hand upward to his nose. There was a cracking sound and a blunt pain in her hand. He cried out, fell back, and grabbed at his gushing nose. She couldn't see Samir or Najah.

"Hellcat," one man said in Arabic.

Zoey wanted to say yes, but kept her mouth shut. It might be to her advantage if they didn't realize she knew Arabic.

Two more men came at her. Zoey kept them back until someone grabbed her from behind. He must have been hiding or waiting out in the emergency exit. Her heart dropped. She'd sent the others out that exit. God, she hoped Catherine, Sara, and Bobbie had listened to her and got away.

"We go, now," the man said, pulling her backward with the other two following. Zoey fought, but he held her tight.

A black van waited, but Zoey was glad to see it was empty. The other women had listened and escaped. At least she hoped so. The man half dragged her and half carried her to a waiting vehicle. Zoey was thrown inside, and they took off.

Zoey reached for the door, but the man grabbed her and tied her hands together with rough rope. She shivered. The men talked quietly, but Zoey picked up several words. The one that bothered her the most was Kalif. Oh, Lord, let Catherine, Bobbie, and Sara all be safe in the palace. She wasn't worth anything to Kalif.

Khalid was going over the parade route with Ryan and the other three sharpshooters when they heard the alarm go off. It was an alarm he'd hoped never to hear, from Malik's office. He took off running for the palace, along with Ryan and several other men. When he got there, the palace was fully lit up, and Malik stood at the door.

"We have a situation." His face was drawn. "Ryan, a taxi will be arriving shortly." Ryan nodded. "Khalid, come inside. The rest of you stay out here."

Khalid followed his brother into his office, where Hassan and Rafi waited, both men with worried looks on their faces.

"What is going on? Why did you sound the alarm?" Khalid asked.

"Wafi's was attacked," Malik said.

Khalid rocked back on his heels. "Attacked? What about the guards? The women?"

Hassan shook his head.

"We don't know." Rafi clasped him on the shoulder. "We just got the information."

"Who is arriving in the taxi?" Khalid asked. Malik had sent Ryan to deal with it. He started for the door.

"Khalid," Malik shouted his name. He stopped and looked back at his brother.

"I'm not sure who is in the taxi. Wafi called and said they'd been attacked, and to expect a taxi."

"That was all he said?" Khalid's heart pounded. What about Zoey? Catherine? Sara and Bobbie? Were they okay? Were they in the car? If so, why didn't Wafi say that? "Their bodyguards?"

"We've lost communication with them," Malik said. Then his phone rang. Malik snatched up the receiver, listened, and then hung up.

"Well?" Three sets of eyes focused in on him.

"Door, now." That was all he said before they all ran for the front door.

The door burst open as they got there. Catherine, Sara, and Bobbie tumbled in. Tears and voices filled the air. Khalid looked around.

"Where the hell is Zoey?" he yelled.

"I'm so sorry, Khalid," Bobbie said, trying to stop crying.

"Family room, now." Malik pulled Catherine with him.

Khalid followed, along with the others. Stay calm, he reminded himself. Yeah, right, the woman he cared about wasn't here where she was safe. His hands clenched at his sides. Getting upset at his sisters-in-law wouldn't accomplish anything.

"This is all my fault," Catherine said as Malik pulled her into his lap.

"No, it's not," Sara said, cuddling up to Hassan.

Rafi held Bobbie close, but they remained standing.

"Zoey?" Khalid asked, again trying to keep from yelling at the top of his lungs.

"We don't know," Bobbie answered.

"You don't know." Khalid couldn't believe his ears. "You're here, but Zoey isn't."

Ryan burst into the room. "The bodyguards have arrived. Wafi's was attacked by Kalif's men."

Khalid's heart stopped. "He has Zoey," he whispered.

"Yes," Ryan said.

"Oh, my God, this is horrible. I'm to blame." Catherine started crying again.

Khalid walked over to Catherine and Malik and knelt. "You are not at fault, sister." He kept his voice soft. As angry as he was, Catherine wasn't to blame. He was. "I allowed you all to be put in danger. Kalif is a maniac, and he'll stop at nothing to get to us." He kicked himself for allowing his feelings to dictate his actions.

"I was the one who planted the idea. I'm responsible."

Malik shook his head, trying to comfort Catherine.

"If anyone is to blame, it is me," Khalid said. "I'm in charge of security." He'd been lulled into lowering his defenses. He'd let his guard down. That wouldn't happen again. Once he got Zoey back, and he would get her back, no matter what, Kalif had to be dealt with. They couldn't afford to let him continue to terrorize everyone. The bodyguards came into the room.

All were battered and bruised, but still standing. Samir stepped forward. "We interrogated one of the musicians. When Kalif heard the women were at Wafi's, he got some of his men to infiltrate the restaurant as musicians."

Khalid stared at Samir. "So it wasn't planned." He wasn't sure if that was a good thing or not. He was barely keeping his emotions in check. Zoey needed him to be strong, and he would do it for her.

"No, sir. It seemed to be a spur-of-the-moment kidnapping." Samir rubbed his bruised cheek. "Hamaz and Habib were outside, Najah and myself inside. They attacked outside first."

Habib stepped forward, rubbing the back of his head. "We didn't even see them coming. One minute everything was fine, the next I was on the ground." Hamaz nodded.

"When they got inside, we fought them," Samir continued.

"I saw Lady Zoey pushed the women toward the hallway," Najah said.

"She pushed us down the hallway to the emergency exit and told us to get out of there," Sara said.

"Why didn't Zoey follow?" Hassan asked.

"I'm not sure," Sara said. "She just yelled at us to get to safety."

Because she'd promised him to keep the others safe. Khalid clenched his teeth. He kicked himself for even letting his guard down for a second and only sending the women with their bodyguards. Yes, the bodyguards were trained, but if a full security force had been there, then Zoey would be safe.

"The musicians," Catherine said. "I remember seeing one of them as we left. Zoey hit him."

"Ryan," Malik yelled.

"I'm already on it."

"What else?" Khalid asked, reining in his impatience.

"The last thing I saw was Zoey standing at the entrance to the hallway," Bobbie said.

"We were so scared. Zoey was so insistent we leave and get to safety. Somehow we found ourselves at the side of the building, and a taxi was at the end of the building. We ran to it and got inside," Sara said.

"You did the right thing," Rafi said.

"Did we?" Catherine asked. "What about Zoey? We shouldn't have left her."

Malik tightened his arms around his wife.

"Convenient the taxi was there. Ryan, is someone interviewing the driver?"

"Yes, Khalid. We're talking to him now to see if he saw anything."

Khalid touched Catherine's arm. He hated seeing her upset. None of this was her fault. "Catherine, my sister, my queen. Had you stayed, you would have been taken too. You did the right thing." In his heart he knew this, even as his head bounced around different scenarios.

"What do we do now?" Catherine asked.

"We wait. Kalif will contact us," Khalid said. It would happen sooner or later, and while they waited he would gather all the information he could.

"I'm going to contact all the tribal leaders and get them together. More eyes out there will help," Malik said.

Khalid looked at Ryan. "I'll go to Wafi's and gather what I can," Ryan said.

"I will go with you," Samir said. "I can show you what I saw."

"You three." Hassan pointed to each woman. "Will go up to your rooms. I'll be by shortly with something to help you rest," Hassan said.

The women began to argue, and Malik stood. "This is not negotiable. Do as Hassan says. That is an order."

Catherine looked mutinous but didn't argue. The women filed out of the room. "Najah, Hamaz, and Habib, do you need a doctor?" Hassan asked.

"No, sir," they answered.

"Good," Malik said. "Go clean up, and we'll let you know the minute we have anything."

The men nodded and left. "Let's go into my office and start planning to rescue Zoey," Malik said.

Zoey grunted as she was shoved into a small tent. "There will be a guard at the entrance. You cannot escape." The man spoke in broken English as he untied her hands and then left.

Zoey looked around. A lantern hung from the center pole. There wasn't much more than a few pillows scattered here and there, a small table, and a cot. Great. No weapons, nothing that could help her. They had switched her from the van to an SUV at one of the villages. She hoped someone in the village had seen them and would report back to Khalid. The ride had been long. Now that her hands were free, she glanced at her watch.

Yep, over four hours. Even thought it was dark, she'd seen that the camp they'd driven into was small. Men gathered around the fire. Not many, and there were only a few tents.

This had to be Kalif's camp. If her sense of direction was right, they were somewhere to the east. She prowled around the tent even as exhaustion grabbed at her. First rules of capture: survive and escape.

She swallowed, having never thought she'd use that little tidbit from the soldiers she'd met in Iraq. As they'd driven, the men had talked in Arabic, unaware she knew the language. She'd learned Catherine, Sara, and Bobbie had escaped. Relief had poured through her. She was thankful for that. She'd kept her promise to Khalid to keep them safe, and Kalif didn't have a royal prisoner.

Just then the tent flap opened, and a small man walked in. His dark hair was pulled back, his beard scruffy, and his clothes dusty. "Well, at least I have one prisoner." He spoke spotless English, though his gravelly voice grated on her nerves.

Zoey glared at him.

"I'm sorry we have to meet under these circumstances. I am Kalif. You are Zoey, the one who has been taking photos and who has been seen with Khalid."

Well, he knew who she was, but then again, she didn't expect anything else. "I don't know why you kidnapped me."

Kalif let out a laugh. "Even though you weren't my first choice, I'm sure my old nemesis Khalid is beside himself with you missing, but there are no worries. I have no intention of hurting you as long as Malik does as I ask."

"And if he doesn't?"

"Then I'm afraid, my dear, you will die."

She shivered as fear slid up her spine, but kept her expression neutral. She wouldn't let the bastard see her reaction to his words. Khalid would find her.

10

Khalid paced around Malik's office. A note had been delivered to the front gate. It had been thoroughly inspected. Khalid had forced himself to let his men do their job and stayed out of their way. He was too emotionally involved. He waited while Malik read the letter.

Malik held the note out to Khalid. He took a deep breath, accepted the note, and read it.

Step down as king, the entire family will give up the throne or I kill the woman. You have twenty-four hours.

Khalid's spine stiffened as his heart pounded. "No fucking way," he murmured. There was no way he'd let Malik give up the throne, let alone let Zoey die.

"It might be the only way to get Zoey back alive," Malik said.

"No." He shook his head. He loved Zoey, but if Malik stepped down it would throw the country into chaos, and that was what Kalif wanted. Chaos.

Khalid froze. He loved Zoey? Of course he did. He'd known for a while. Now to find a way to get the love of his life back without his brother giving up the throne. "Get Hassan and Rafi in here. Maybe Rafi has a contact who can tell us where Kalif is."

Malik frowned at him but called in his brothers. They were both incensed that Kalif had been so brazen, but also just as insistent that Malik not step down.

"Khalid thinks you might know someone who can help us, Rafi," Malik said.

"I already tried." He glanced at Malik. "I had an informant who was feeding me information on Kalif, but even he doesn't know where Kalif moved his camp to. He did tell me that Kalif is down to about twenty men," Rafi said.

"Now what?" Hassan asked. "He's only given us twenty-four hours."

Khalid was tempted to say he'd tear the country apart in those twenty-four hours, but it wasn't possible. "He has to still be in the east; he isn't going to stray far from his last poppy field."

Malik reached for the map rolled up behind his desk and spread it out. They'd been using it to pinpoint the poppy fields as they got rid of them.

"Shit," Khalid muttered.

"What?" Malik raised his head.

"The tracker. I forgot all about it." Khalid grabbed the phone and told Jahir to get up there with his computer.

Jahir arrived and sat his computer on Malik's desk where they could all see. "The device was working, sir."

"Was?" Khalid's gut clenched.

"We weren't sure of the range, but based on the last ping of the device, it looks like Lady Zoey was taken east. Let me bring up the satellite map."

"Why didn't I think about this earlier?" Khalid was angry with himself.

"Maybe because we haven't used them before? Even I forgot." Malik rubbed his brother's shoulder.

"Here we go," Jahir said. "She was here." He pointed with his mouse to the map.

Khalid stared at the image on the computer. All he could see was dunes and mountains in the distance. Mountains? "He's close to the border," he muttered. Kalif could escape across the border, and they'd lose him.

Malik's phone rang. He picked it up and listened. "Yes, have Ryan bring them up." He hung up the receiver. "The tribal leaders heard what happened. Two of them are here with information."

A few minutes later, Ryan escorted Faruq and Bassam into Malik's office. Malik motioned them to the empty chairs as the brothers stood.

"King Malik," they both said, and then they sat.

"How did you hear so quickly? I only sent my message an hour ago." Malik asked.

"Anwar happened to be at Wafi's, and he saw what happened. He came to us and we put out feelers," Faruq said.

"We are enraged Kalif would kidnap Lady Zoey," Bassam said.

"And we need to find her," Khalid said, then looked at Malik who nodded. "Malik received a note from Kalif. If Malik doesn't give up the throne, and the rest of us renounce the throne, Kalif will kill Zoey."

Both men gasped. "No, that is unacceptable. It is a good thing we have information." Bassam glanced at the computer sitting on Malik's desk. "Kalif's camp is here." He pointed to an area about three miles due east of where they'd lost Zoey's tracking device.

Rafi swore. It was the area they'd been looking at the last few months. Very open land.

"There is no way to sneak up on them," Hassan said.

"Unless," Khalid said, opening the map Malik had and running his finger over it, "we take SUVs out this far." He pointed to a place on the map. "Then continue on foot."

"It will take time," Rafi said.

"Yes, it's at least a couple hours' hike. My Zoey is strong, she'll hang on until we get there. If we take off now, we can be there by dawn," Khalid said. He refused to see any other outcome other than rescuing Zoey.

"King Malik," Bassam said. "If you need help, the tribal leaders are willing."

Khalid shook his head. He didn't want anyone but his own men involved. He didn't want a bystander hurt and, while he trusted Bassam, he didn't know or trust all his men.

"We appreciate the offer," Malik said. "We don't want any of the tribal leaders injured."

Bassam nodded. "Kalif won't give up easily."

"Tell us something we don't know," Rafi muttered.

After going over the area with the two tribal leaders, the two men left, and Khalid sent Ryan and Jahir off to get the security force ready.

"I'm going with you," Rafi said.

"No." He stared at his brother. "I know you want to help, Rafi, but if anything goes wrong, I don't want you to be captured."

"Yet you're risking yourself," Hassan commented.

"For the woman I love, yes." Saying the words aloud strengthened his resolve. His brothers stared at him, then each nodded.

"How about Rafi and I stay at the clinic here?" Hassan pointed to the village. It was close to a two-hour drive from where Kalif was, but they'd be safe.

"I want your word, no matter what happens, you'll stay at the village." He didn't want his brothers risking their lives.

They nodded, not that he believed them. If they thought he was at risk, they'd run to the rescue.

"Malik, check with the minister of Qasim and get us a helicopter or two." Their neighbor to the east would be open to helping, and this way he could get Zoey back to the palace quicker.

"Yes. I'll ask him to keep them on standby for your call." Malik checked his watch. "I know you won't be able to check in often, but if you can at least let me know when you've arrived outside Kalif's camp and are getting ready to attack. Catherine, Sara, and Bobbie are not going to be happy."

Khalid nodded. "I'll do my best. Hassan and Rafi, I suggest you talk with Sara and Bobbie before you go; otherwise, they'll be upset." He didn't want the women to worry, just like he wouldn't want Zoey to worry if the situation were different.

"Agreed," Hassan said.

"We'll leave in an hour." Khalid turned and left the room. There was a lot to get done, including preparing himself. Because there was no way he'd let Zoey be killed. He'd rather die himself.

~

Zoey rubbed her forehead as she lay on the cot. She'd dozed in and out for most of the night. Kalif had entered the tent before dawn with a gleam in his eye. He informed her he'd sent a message to Malik and awaited his answer. If he didn't get one by tonight, then she would die.

Damn. The man was insane. She could only imagine what Khalid and his family were going through. She was scared, but she could imagine what Catherine, Sara, and Bobbie were feeling. They'd all become friends, and she hated they were hurting because of her. Thank goodness she'd gotten them out of Wafi's, and they were safe. If Kalif had taken all of them—a shudder wracked her body. No, it was better that it was just her. She could handle this.

One of Kalif's men had brought her water and food a bit ago. She wasn't hungry, but she ate anyway. She needed to keep her strength up. Then she stretched out her sore muscles and walked around the tent.

It wasn't going to be pleasant staying in the tent all day, but she would endure anything to give Khalid time to find her. And of that she was sure. She wasn't sure if the tracker still worked, but at least they'd have something to go on. He wouldn't give up. Of course, she might be dead by then.

Zoey shook her head. No use thinking that way. Her focus must be on escape, and if not her own, at least to be a help to any rescue.

A sliver of light caught her eye. She found the source of the light. There was a loose panel in the tent's construction. If she could work the panel until it was open, then maybe she could escape. She'd have to be careful and not get caught. She smiled for the first time in hours, ever so grateful she'd paid attention to her military friends.

Khalid took a deep breath as he lay down on the hill slightly above Kalif's camp. The other two sharpshooters were moving into positions closer to the camp. He didn't trust anyone but himself to be the primary shooter. Zoey's life was at stake. He pulled out his rifle and attached the scope. At his command, Ryan and the others would invade the camp. He would be here ready to take out anyone who threatened Zoey.

It had taken them longer to get to the camp than anticipated. They'd made it just after dawn, but needed to wait to attack. Khalid and Ryan had discussed with the others the best time to attack. Sunset. Luckily, they had plenty of supplies, including water.

He'd watched Kalif's men for the last thirty minutes. The men moved around the camp slowly. There was a lack of sharpness to their movements. Their shoulders slumped, and their steps were hesitant. Kalif's men all seemed worn out. Or maybe they were tired of following Kalif.

He hated having to leave Zoey there all day, but there wasn't much he could do about it. He only hoped they were giving her food and water. His heart pounded as he settled into position.

Thinking of the past and the consequences were not in Zoey's best interest. Today would be different, because today he must save the woman he loved. There could be no mistakes. It seemed like forever, but finally, the sun began to sink. Khalid calmed his body, ready for anything.

Zoey finished untying the flap at the back of the tent about noon. It was big enough she could slip out. She'd stuck her head through a few times to get the lay of the land, but was very careful not to be seen or make any noise. The camp had been fairly quiet all day. Food and water had been brought to her this morning, but that was it.

She listened to the men outside her tent grumble about Kalif. They were worried Kalif was out for more of his own gain than anything else. She wanted to talk to them, convince them to help her escape, but remained worried they'd turn on her. Instead, she planned her escape. She used the heat as an excuse to push the front flap open, and she sat at the opening.

This way she could watch what the men were doing, which wasn't much. She got an idea of how many men were in camp, where the other tents were positioned, and where the vehicles and horses were. She could ride if she needed to.

When the sun was the hottest, she closed the flap, commenting she was going to nap. Instead, she slipped out the back. She didn't go far, just a few feet. Enough to scope out where she could run when the time came. And it was going to come soon. She slipped back inside the tent as a sweet, almost sickly flowery smell began to permeate the air. Zoey heard yelling, and she went to the entrance of the tent to listen.

"The prince is here. They're burning the poppy field."

The words were spoken in Arabic, and Zoey had never in her life been so grateful she understood the language. Now, she would wait and watch. Khalid would be there soon, and she would do everything she could to help him.

"Kalif wants us to stay here and guard the prisoner."

"Where is Kalif?"

"Preparing."

"For what?"

"The time has passed for King Malik and the family to abdicate. Kalif is going to kill the woman."

Zoey stumbled back. So that was what Kalif wanted from Malik. There was no way Malik would abdicate the throne unless Kalif had grabbed Catherine. So that had been the plan, and she'd ruined it. Good. Quietly, she made her way to the back of the tent and waited. She had to pick just the right time; otherwise, this would be over before it started. She wasn't about to let some madman kill her, not without a fight.

Khalid watched his men set fire to the poppy field, then trained his sight back on the camp. Kalif hadn't shown his face yet, but his men were pacing and kept their guns close. They seemed worried, and they should be. His men were about to storm the camp and find Zoey. Anyone who tried to stop them would suffer the consequences.

"We're ready," Ryan said, his voice coming through loud and clear on the earpiece.

"Mic's open and go," was all Khalid said. He kept his sight trained on the tent where he he'd seen Zoey earlier.

~

Zoey heard shouts and then gunfire. Time to make her getaway. She slipped the back tent flap open and stuck her head out to make sure the coast was clear, then she slipped out. She turned, and one of Kalif's men rounded the tent. He stopped when he saw her and pulled a knife from his sash.

Zoey held her breath. She could fight, but against a knife it wouldn't be easy. Maybe she could keep him busy enough for Khalid or one of his men to find them.

The man flipped the knife around and held it out to her handle first. Zoey hesitated, and he lifted it toward her. "Protect yourself," he whispered in English.

With a slight hesitation, she reached out and grasped the handle. The man let go, then tossed her the scabbard. Then, with a nod, he ran past her. She put the knife into the holder, and slipped it into the side pocket of her pants. She could reach it there, but it wouldn't be visible to others. She edged her way to the end of the tent and peeked around. Kalif's men were running all over the place, yelling and shouting.

Could she make a run for it? Maybe? They looked disorganized. But she didn't want to bring attention to herself. She ran to the next tent and made her way around it, away from prying eyes.

Her heart pounded, but she forced her breathing to remain calm. Panicking wouldn't help right now. She needed to find Khalid or one of his men and get the hell out of here. She'd just peeked around the tent when she was grabbed from behind.

"Sneaky bitch."

The rough tone, stinky smell, and the knife to her throat made her aware Kalif had her. Damn it.

"Now, I show Khalid what happens when he attacks me." He marched her out from behind the tent, and Zoey grit her teeth. She wouldn't go down without a fight. She wasn't going to let this madman get the best of her or Khalid.

~

Khalid blinked as he saw Kalif, using Zoey as a shield, come out from between the tents. "Ryan, to your left about thirty feet. He's got Zoey."

"Roger that."

Khalid fought to keep his breathing even and his hands steady. He didn't have a shot at Kalif, not yet. There were so many variables, but he refused to let his mind dwell on those. He would save the woman he loved.

"Be alert everyone. If you have a clean shot at Kalif, shout out," he said. He had no choice now but to trust others.

"Negative on shot." The other two sharpshooters replied.

Damn. Ryan and his men had dispatched Kalif's men quickly, either tying them up or leaving them unconscious as they moved toward Kalif and Zoey. Half of his men split off and started to circle.

"Where is he?" Kalif yelled as Ryan came to a stop about twenty feet from him. Kalif's rough voice came out loud and clear through Ryan's mic. Khalid was able to hear everything.

"I'm all you have," Ryan said.

"Get him here. I want him to see his woman die."

"Not going to happen," Khalid muttered. "Come on, baby, move your head just a little." Zoey was in the line of fire, and he wouldn't take any chances with her. "Keep him talking, Ryan. I don't have a shot."

"Come on, Kalif. You don't want to die."

Kalif let out a laugh. "Do you really think he'll let me live?"

"Khalid is not a killer," Zoey said.

"Shut up." Kalif tightened his grip on her.

Khalid fought to breathe. If the knife slipped or his shot missed ... No, he wouldn't think about that. He blocked out the voices and zeroed in on his target.

Zoey's arm moved. What was she doing?

Zoey inched her fingers to her side pocket and began easing the knife from its place. She was only going to have one shot at this. Khalid had to be watching from the scope on his sniper's gun. That would be the only reason he wasn't here in front of her.

They'd spoken at night in bed about his time with the UK special forces, not that he said much, just how he was a sharpshooter and, while he'd kept up with his skill, he only used it on very rare and needed occasions. If there was ever a time for him to use his special skill, it was now.

Kalif kept her positioned very carefully, so Zoey knew she would have to make a bold move. Ryan didn't take his eyes off Kalif as she pulled the knife free. She closed her eyes and sent a quick prayer, then plunged the knife into Kalif's leg.

He roared in pain, and the arm around her neck dropped. Zoey dropped to the ground, and a shot sounded. She felt the thunk of someone falling before Ryan was at her side.

"Zoey, are you all right?" He half lifted her off the ground.

"I'm ... " Her head was spinning, and her heart was pounding. She'd never stabbed a man before. She glanced behind her to see Kalif lying in the sand with a hole in his head and the knife sticking out of his leg, blood flowing.

"Zoey," Khalid yelled as he slid to his knees in front of her, his gun thrown over his back with a strap across his chest. He was breathing hard, and she realized he must have run flat out from his position.

"I'm fine," she whispered as she looked at his worried face. Her eyes filled with tears, and then suddenly she was sobbing.

Khalid pulled Zoey into his arms as she cried. "Zoey, honey."

"It's the shock of everything, Khalid," Ryan said. "The SUVs should be here within the hour. Unless you want to call in the helicopter?" A blanket was produced and thrown over her. "Let's take her away from this." Ryan waved his hand at Kalif's body.

Khalid nodded. Ryan slipped the sniper rifle from his back, and helped Khalid to his feet. Khalid carried her to the edge of the camp, and then sat down in the shade provided by one of the tents. Ryan set his rifle next to him and then left them alone.

"I've got you, baby." He rubbed her back. "No one will ever hurt you again," he whispered against her ear as he held her close.

~

"I'm fine. I really am," Zoey said two days later, as Catherine, Sara, and Bobbie entered her room to find her sitting at her computer.

She actually couldn't blame the women for wanting to see her and wait on her. When Khalid had arrived back with her, Hassan had taken over. She'd been in shock, but also mildly dehydrated. She'd been put to bed and given a mild sedative.

Hassan wanted to take her to the hospital, but Khalid vetoed it. Instead, he stayed with her, making her drink every time she woke up for the first twelve hours. For the next forty-eight hours he refused to leave her side. She'd finally got him to leave her a few hours ago, so he could shower, change, and talk with Malik. The lines of strain were apparent on his face.

It didn't matter. She had told him she would be fine, but apparently he'd sent the women to check on her and make sure she didn't overdo it.

"Shouldn't you be in bed?" Bobbie said.

"It's good she's up and moving around," Sara said.

"I can't believe you stabbed Kalif," Catherine said.

"Catherine," Bobbie and Sara shouted.

Zoey smiled. "It's all right." She'd come to terms with what she'd done. From the time she'd spent in Iraq, she was aware not everything was black and white. The choice had been to stab Kalif or let him kill her. She'd made the decision to go out fighting, and she had.

The women sat down. "Ryan told us what happened," Catherine said.

Zoey nodded. The entire drive back to the palace, she'd been aware of Ryan's gaze, the approval in it. Habib had made sure the blanket stayed wrapped around her while giving Khalid water for her to drink.

Now she was feeling like her old self. But there were things she needed to get out of her head, and she found writing them down really helped. She'd kept an electronic journal for so long it was habit, but today she really needed it.

So as the women talked, she typed, and typed, and typed. She was good at multitasking, keeping up with the conversation and typing. By the time Zoey was finished, she had more than twenty pages, and the women were calling for food.

Sara walked up to Zoey. "All typed out, now?"

Zoey looked up at her. "Better."

"Good." Sara touched Zoey shoulder. "If you have any nightmares, or issues with sleeplessness, fear, super alertness, or anything out of the ordinary, please don't keep it to yourself. If you don't want to tell Khalid or Hassan, come to me."

Gratitude filled Zoey. "Thank you, Sara." Zoey stood and hugged Sara.

"What happened to you was a trauma, and I don't want you to suffer."

"Honestly, I think what I saw and experienced was worse in Iraq, but I do appreciate the offer. I'm worried about Khalid."

"Why?"

"He took a life. That has to weigh heavily on him." Did Sara not know about what happened in the UK? Had Khalid not told anyone but her? It was possible. The man was tight- lipped about certain things.

"He'll talk to Hassan."

"Food is here," Catherine said as she opened the door.

Four hours later, Zoey found Khalid in the garden. "You should be resting," he said when he saw her.

"I've rested enough." She walked into his open arms. "I think you could use some sleep." She ran her fingers over the lines of tiredness creasing his handsome features.

He shook his head. "When I close my eyes, all I see is that knife to your throat."

"I'm safe. We're both safe." Zoey ran her hands over his back. "Have you talked to Hassan?"

He shook his head. Zoey stepped back and led him over to the bench. "You aren't sleeping, you've never slept well. Khalid, you have to let someone help you." She kept her arms around him.

"I can't," he whispered.

"You can." She rubbed his back. "What happened wasn't your fault."

"My head says that's true, but my heart … " He rubbed his chest.

"Khalid," Zoey said, placing her hand over his.

"My Zoey," he said, his forehead coming to rest against hers. "I love you."

He loved her. She inhaled. Her heart squeezed. "Oh, Khalid. I love you too." There, she'd said the words. It was a relief to finally tell him of her love.

His dark eyes flared with heat. "You love me."

"Of course I do."

"But I overheard Bobbie and Catherine talking about your leaving?"

"Yes. Khalid, I didn't want to burden you with my wanderlust. You understand why I can't sit still."

"I do, but there has to be a way."

"How? You're a prince, part of the royal family. They need you. You're head of security."

"I need you."

"As I do you." She shook her head. "Let's not talk about this now. Tomorrow is the anniversary parade." It had been delayed a few days because of her kidnapping and rescue. "You can't let down the people of Bashir."

He shook his head. "My Zoey, always thinking of others."

Zoey wandered around the crowds for the parade, snapping pictures. Her lips curved into a smile. The people loved the royal family. Khalid had wanted her with him, but she finally convinced him to let her take her pictures among the crowd.

A float went by with the peace symbol, and the crowd cheered. Khalid had told her that one of the elders had told his grandson about the peace sign being used as a symbol for the people to resist. The grandson had told his friends. They were the ones who were painting it on the buildings, to give the people a symbol.

Habib was right beside her. Ryan and the others were protecting the family, but with Kalif dead, everyone was more relaxed. She stopped and took pictures as the parade went by. She was allowed to be on the edge of the street so she could take her pictures. Habib made sure of that. Being able to be here so close was a rare chance to photograph a parade in a small Middle-Eastern country. Her shutter constantly clicked, the viewfinder rarely more than a fraction of an inch from her eye.

As the float with the royal family came into view, Zoey pointed her lens toward them and zoomed, finger pressed to the shutter. She moved between them and the people. This was going to make for a feel-good article. Her stomach clenched.

She would be leaving soon. She couldn't stay, as much as she wanted to. Maybe in ten years or so, she'd be able to settle down in one place, but she couldn't ask Khalid to wait that long. She loved him, and she was willing to let him go. It wasn't fair to make him choose between his duty and her.

The crowd grew louder as the royal family's float moved closer. Zoey took picture after picture. Later she'd put them all together and smile. She stayed in front of the float until Habib put a hand on her arm.

"Habib?"

"Wait, Lady Zoey."

She turned to see Khalid jump off the float and stride over to her. The crowd went wild. He took her hands in his. "We have a solution, but more about that later. Right now." He knelt before she could question him.

Zoey's heart pounded. What was he doing? "Lady Zoey Lacey, will you do me the honor of being my wife?"

Zoey's eyes widened. "Ummm." He was proposing? In front of everyone? After her telling him she couldn't stay? Her stomach clenched.

"Trust me," he whispered.

"I do," she whispered back. The crowd grew quiet. She gathered her courage. She was going to let her heart speak for once. "Yes, Khalid. I'll marry you," she said in a loud voice.

The crowd went crazy. Khalid stood, scooped her up into his arms, and climbed back aboard the float. Everyone was clapping, and Catherine had tears in her eyes.

Sara beamed, and Bobbie almost jumped up and down. The men just looked pleased.

"Now, you ride with the family. Because you have always been a part of us." Khalid lowered his head and took her lips with his. Zoey melted into the kiss and his arms. His plan better be good, because she didn't want her heart broken.

Later that evening, they finally made it back to the palace. Zoey entered the family room to see Khalid standing by the bar. Otherwise, the room was empty. She walked over to him, and he drew her into his arms.

"Khalid, today was magical, but it changes nothing. You know I love you, and I love your control in the bedroom, but I can't give up my work. Not after my parents." He had to understand.

"Baby, I know." He drew her closer, resting his forehead on hers.

"I've found a way you don't have to leave," Malik said, entering the room.

Zoey turned within Khalid's hold. "What do you mean?"

"Khalid told me about your need not to feel hemmed in," Malik said. "Not like any of us hadn't noticed." He grinned. "It took a bit of work, but there is a solution."

Zoey's heart lightened. "There is? What is it?"

"How would you like to be Bashir's official international ambassador?" Malik asked.

"International ambassador?" She tilted her head to the side.

"Yes, your translations skills are something we need, and as our international ambassador you would still be able to travel," Malik said.

"But Khalid?"

"I'll be with you every step of the way." He tightened his arms around her waist.

"How?"

"Between Ryan and the others, they can protect the family while I'm gone. Habib and I will be with you."

"And now that Kalif is gone," Malik said, "we really don't have that many security issues. The tribal leaders are happy to take over the area where Kalif was growing poppies and make the land profitable for livestock."

"Khalid?" Zoey looked up at him. "Are you sure about this?"

"I love you, and I don't want to lose you. This way we both get what we want. And you can continue with your blog and travel articles, there are plenty of countries that want to work with us."

"I've had requests pouring in for months. You're going to be very busy," Malik said, then he turned and left the room.

Zoey turned to Khalid. "You're really sure about this?" She could scarcely believe it.

"Yes." He brushed a kiss over her nose. "I took your advice."

"What was that?"

"I talked with Hassan about what happened in the UK. With Kalif gone, the imminent threat to the family is gone. I can now concentrate on myself a bit. I trust Ryan and the others. They've been trained well and know how to do their jobs." He leaned back. "Besides, no one but me is going to guard the woman I love."

Zoey laughed. "I guess that means I better learn how to be an ambassador."

"You'll do great." He grinned at her. "You convinced me within minutes of meeting you, you were the woman for me."

He covered her lips with his. She was where she wanted to be. In the arms of the man she loved.

EPILOGUE

ONE YEAR LATER

Zoey let out a breath as she surveyed the room. The year from the anniversary parade to her wedding had been a busy one. True to his word, Malik had made her Bashir's international ambassador, and the requests had come pouring in.

Bashir itself prospered during the year as well. They were selling crops and animals to other countries. Exports and imports were at an all-time high. The marketplace was always bustling with people and tourists.

She smiled. Four royal weddings would do that. She glanced around the room and found her husband talking with Ryan. She shook her head. He couldn't stop being who he was in terms of security.

Her husband. She looked down at the gold band on her finger. Earlier today he'd placed it on her finger, and they'd said their vows. The people of Bashir had gone all out for their wedding. She'd been surprised when her parents had attended her wedding and her father had walked her down the aisle. But they were already on their way back to their hotel, refusing to stay in the palace.

Now, she wanted to escape with Khalid and have some quiet time together. Between traveling and the preparations for the wedding, she was ready for a little downtime.

"They make one heck of group of handsome men," Sara said, coming up next to her.

"They do." Ryan had left, and Khalid's brothers had joined him. All of them stood there decked out in their royal colors.

"You were a beautiful bride," Catherine said, dabbing at her eyes.

"Don't cry again," Zoey said. Catherine had been crying off and on all day.

"She can't help it," Bobbie said joining the group.

"Did you get Zain to bed?" Six months ago, the adoption of Zain had come through for Bobbie and Rafi. The little boy was still coming out of his shell, but today he'd run around and played with the other children at the reception.

"Yes, he fell right asleep."

"I could take a nap myself," Catherine sniffled, and Zoey was worried.

"Catherine, is there something wrong?" Zoey asked. Just then the men shouted.

"Well, I guess Malik told them," Catherine said and smiled. "I'm pregnant."

"Congratulations. That is fantastic," Zoey said, and the women all hugged.

The men sauntered over. "I guess she told you," Malik said, slipping his arm around his wife's waist.

"She did," Sara said, taking her place at Hassan's side. "I'm so happy for you."

"Me too," Bobbie said.

"We picked good women," Rafi said, pulling Bobbie into his arms.

"We did." Khalid put his arms around Zoey's waist and pulled her back against his body. Heat filled her.

"So, Sara, you're next," Catherine said.

Sara's face flushed. "Not just yet. You and Malik needed an heir. Hassan and I can take our time."

"Yes, it's fun practicing," Hassan said.

The group laughed when Sara looked outraged at Hassan's words, but then she laughed too.

"Now that all of us are married, and Bashir is prospering, what shall we accomplish next?" Malik asked.

"I think you all deserve some time off," a male voice said.

They turned to see Jamal and Anna at the door, grinning ear to ear.

"I thought you two were on your way back to the summer palace," Khalid said. His parents had attended their wedding but wanted to get back to the summer palace where they were now living.

"We were," Anna said gliding into the room. "Then we decided that we should spend a few days here while all of you took some time off."

"Time off, what is that?" Hassan asked.

Everyone laughed. It was rare any of them took more than a day off from their duties. Not that any of them complained.

"Starting now, everyone is off duty. Ryan will take care of security. The hospital will take care of itself. The stable hands have everything covered, and I'll take care of the country," Jamal said.

Malik started to protest, but Jamal held his hand up, silencing his son. "I'll contact you if I need you, but for the next thirty-six hours I want all of you to spend time together with your wives."

"On that note, what do you say we leave and have our own party?" Khalid whispered in her ear.

Heat flowed through her veins. "Sounds good."

Khalid walked them backward out of the room. She'd like to believe that no one noticed, but everyone was grinning. They were at the bottom of the stairs when she heard Anna yell, "Baby."

"I guess they told her," Zoey said, smiling up at her husband.

"Yes." He swept her into his arms. "Now, let us go work on our own baby."

Her heart swelled, filled with love and laughter and a sense of belonging.

ACKNOWLEDGMENTS

Always to my critique group who support me

ABOUT THE AUTHOR

Marie Tuhart lives in the beautiful Pacific Northwest with her muse, Penny, a four-pound toy poodle. Marie loves to read and write. When she's not writing, she spends time with family, traveling and enjoying life.

Marie is a multi-published author with The Wild Rose Press, Trifecta Publishing House and does some self-publishing. To be alerted on new releases you can join Marie's newsletter where she gives her group advance information on her books, runs contests and does give-aways just for newsletter readers. Marie can also be found on Pinterest, Twitter, and Facebook.